"I want to hear how you did on the run," Hudson said.

"More important, I want to hear how you're doing on the inside."

His incredible eyes had turned darker than usual. Shannon couldn't hold his gaze any longer. He was back to the things of the heart again. He was a great coach and she wouldn't have gotten this far without him, but for him it wasn't about winning.

"The mountain, the sky, the hill and the speed… It was glorious.…" She let her words trail off.

Hudson locked eyes with her, his gaze reflecting the wonder of the passion for skiing they shared. He believed in her.

Encouraged, she continued pouring out the experience, describing every twist and turn of the run. How she felt more in control than she had in a long time. Except for the one thorn behind her kneecap, but she kept that part to herself.

"And when I reached the end, all I could think was that I'm back." *Oh, please let me be back. Let me convince him.*

She dared to look into Hudson's eyes.

Books by Elizabeth Goddard

Love Inspired Heartsong Presents

Love in the Air
Love on the Slopes

Love Inspired Suspense

Freezing Point
Treacherous Skies
Riptide
Wilderness Peril

ELIZABETH GODDARD

is an award-winning author with well over a dozen romance and romantic suspense novels, including the romantic mystery *The Camera Never Lies*—winner of the prestigious Carol Award in 2011. After acquiring her computer science degree, she worked at a software firm before eventually retiring to raise her four children and become a professional writer. A member of several writing organizations, she judges numerous contests and mentors new writers. In addition to writing, she homeschools her children and serves with her husband as he pastors a church in Louisiana.

ELIZABETH GODDARD

Love on the Slopes

HEARTSONG
PRESENTS

™ LOVE INSPIRED BOOKS

Recycling programs for this product may not exist in your area.

ISBN-13: 978-0-373-48690-8

LOVE ON THE SLOPES

www.Harlequin.com

Printed in U.S.A.

How great is the love the Father has lavished on us, that we should be called children of God! And that is what we are! The reason the world does not know us is that it did not know him.

—*John* 3:1

Dedicated to my Lord and Savior Jesus Christ,
who loves me unconditionally.

Acknowledgments

I couldn't do this without my family and friends,
who understand the time required to write
and edit my novels. Special thanks to Katya Franzgen
and Brett Maul of the Adaptive Ski Program
in Santa Fe for their assistance.

Chapter 1

Winning was everything.

Shannon de Croix stabbed her ski poles into the packed snow just in front of the starting gate.

If she placed first at one or more events at the nationals, it would bump her up in the rankings. Just one of many stepping-stones to put her in line for a nomination to the U.S. Ski Team. A dream that had already eluded her for far too long.

Focusing on the downhill course ahead of her, she sucked in a breath, the scent of evergreens, winter and fresh-fallen snow filling her nostrils, exhilarating her.

Shannon had practically been born on skis. She could do this. The downhill race wasn't anything she hadn't done a thousand times before, but on other hills and in other competitions. The only difference—this was a big race.

An important race.

The downhill event was all about speed. No skiing around gates. Nothing she couldn't handle, except, normally, she would have been allowed to examine the course ahead of time. Shannon never thought she'd rue the day it snowed, but the extreme weather had forced a delay in the race, leaving all the competitors to ski at a disadvantage. Skiing the course a day or two before the race was part of getting prepared, and there was nothing more important than being prepared—her dad had ingrained that rule in her since the start of her ski career.

Ignoring this rule grated just under her skin. She needed to be in sync with the mountain. But she wasn't alone in this—her opponents were at the same disadvantage. No one, not even their coaches or staff, had been allowed on the course.

The signal came. None of that mattered now. She had ten seconds before the start.

Zeroing in on the course, she stared ahead, shoving aside the doubts and the fact she would fly down a mountain at breakneck speed on a slope she wasn't completely familiar with. In the roped-off starting area, race officials edged her vision, along with other skiers waiting their turn and Jack—the team captain, who watched her. The two of them were more than simply members of the same ski team. They shared the same dreams, the same aspirations, and Shannon was on the verge of losing her heart completely to the guy.

Next to him stood Coach Hudson Landers—the man who'd brought them this far.

The clock ticked as Shannon steadied her breathing, shoving all thoughts from her mind save one.

Ski hard. Ski fast.

The starter counted down the last five seconds.

Five, four, three, two... The blast of a horn signaled the start of the race. In an instant, Shannon pressed her weight into her poles and leaned forward, pushing off onto the downhill slope, gaining momentum by skating on her skis for the first few feet.

She picked up speed as gravity and the slick bottom of her racing skis propelled her forward.

Faster.

Racing down the hill at more than 80 mph, cold air pricking her cheeks, Shannon slipped into that place where she performed best and became one with the mountain. Everything around her a blur, time seemed to stand still. The familiar whoosh of the skis slicking through the crisp snow enveloped her, kept her focused on one thing ahead of her—the finish line.

At the top of her game, the doubts drifted away with each passing second. She prepared for a rise in the course, braced her knees for the jump and took to the air. The ground was fast approaching, and she readied for impact.

Hitting the snow-packed slope, her left leg slipped to the side, and the ground flew at her face. She raised her arms to protect herself and kept tumbling. Pain spiked through her hard and fast. Screams erupted somewhere around her. They were her own.

The blue sky finally stopped spinning and twisting with the evergreens and snow. She stared up. Seconds ticked by before she could draw in a breath. Could she move? Was she paralyzed?

Please, no...

Shannon flailed her arms and lifted her head. But moving her legs caused pain to sear through her. She cried out, reaching for her leg, her knee. Was it a catastrophic injury that could end her career, her dreams?

Emergency officials appeared. *Jack, where are you?*

There. He was there. He reached for her hand, pity filling his gaze. No, she didn't want pity. "Jack?"

"Don't worry, Shannon. You'll be back with us. You

have to," he said, then disappeared when the officials pushed him aside.

Hudson's face came into view then, his encouraging smile failing to hide his concern. "I'm right here, Shannon. I'm not going anywhere."

But his words didn't soothe her. No. Jack's words rang in her mind instead. Suspicions swirled inside her. Didn't he care about *her?* Was it all about the race? But she knew. She *knew.* He would go on.

Without her.

Every bit of confidence and determination threatened to deflate. She'd never been one to quit. Always a winner, always a fighter, but this time, Shannon couldn't help it. She succumbed to the awful possibility that, just like that, her future was over.

February, Ridgewood Ski Lodge
Sangre de Cristo Mountains, New Mexico

The snowflakes fell thick and heavy on the ski slopes. Wanting to look his students in the eyes, Hudson shoved his goggles over his helmet.

He stood with the junior members of the Ridgewood Ski Team, ages eight to twelve, at the top of Windstorm, one of several blue, or intermediate-level, ski runs. Just one of many at Ridgewood Ski Lodge.

Hudson started to speak, but one of the students interrupted and pointed behind him. "Hey, Coach Landers, I thought you told Shannon not to ski Terminator."

Hudson glanced at the ski lift that started at the top of this run and had only one destination. Just disappearing from his sight, Shannon sat in the chairlift, her auburn hair and turquoise ski suit giving her away. She likely figured he would be too busy to notice.

Terminator, the double-black-diamond ski run and

Ridgewood's biggest draw, boasted mind-bending vertical drops and an unrivaled obstacle-course terrain. Terminator could be skied only by experts.

Skillful skiers who were in their best condition, not rehabilitating from a serious injury.

Grinding his molars, Hudson reined in his frustration and concern for the girl, and faced the group of much younger aspiring athletes, hoping they wouldn't follow her example when it came to his instructions.

All eyes watched him, waiting for his explanation. He pointed a finger at the boy. "Don't eavesdrop on my conversations." To the group as a whole, he said, "Shannon knows what she's doing."

They visibly relaxed, trusting his words, but he couldn't say the same.

If only their coach wasn't a dream killer. That was what Shannon had said to him when, moments before, he'd told her it was too soon for Terminator.

Hudson sighed—he'd hoped coaching, helping others achieve their dreams, would somehow erase his mistakes. Redeem his past.

Who was he kidding?

He had no power to make dreams come true. Sometimes they were elusive—just out of reach. Other times they crashed and never got up. Hudson knew all about the death of a dream, and he knew about killing someone else's, too. He'd done it once before, and he carried the weight of it with him every day.

Coaching a ski team should have saved him, eased his burdens.

Instead he'd made a bad call, and Shannon had taken a career-changing fall. He was her coach. He'd made the decision to ski even though they hadn't been able to inspect the course.

But thirteen sets of eyes peered at him now, bringing

him back to the moment. After giving his instructions to his students, he radioed for Travis—one of the six Ridgewood coaches—to start the video.

The skiers took off down the run, and Hudson skied behind them between the gates he'd set up earlier. As head coach for the past two years, he typically worked with the older students who already had a great foundation but were ready to make a name for themselves in competitive racing. Today, he covered for assistant coach Jason Hawkins while the man was on his honeymoon. Hudson had looked forward to working with the younger age group again—feel what it was like to inspire them.

Or maybe he hoped inspiring them would ignite his own passions again and give him a reason to stay at Ridgewood and continue to coach. But his time with them was nearly over, and he knew now what he'd tried to ignore—he wouldn't be able to be passionate about the sport again until he somehow freed himself from his past.

As they raced down the slope toward the Ridgewood Ski Lodge, Hudson glanced up at the snowy peaks across the snow-covered plateau opposite Mount Monroe, or Momentum to the locals, the mountain on which he now skied. The ski crowd had grown since he had started with the students. Ridgewood was close enough to Santa Fe so that, in addition to the ski junkies on a getaway weekend, local enthusiasts could drive up for an afternoon jaunt on the slopes.

Drawing in a breath of crisp air, he watched the kids while he slowly skied behind. This group had an upcoming fun race in a couple of weeks. He could already see the potential in some, and he knew they would go far. But it required more than talent—they needed the fire to race. The drive to win.

And the racing circuit could be brutal.

At the bottom of the hill, the thirteen kids came to a perfect stop, just like they'd been taught, and Hudson smiled.

He whooshed in front of the group, sending snow into their faces, and earned a few laughs. Each of their expressions shone with exhilaration and hard work.

He tugged his goggles up and onto his head again so they could look into his eyes. "We're good for today. We'll view the video on Saturday. See you this weekend."

The junior team practiced once a week and on weekends, depending on the level. The Ridgewood coaches had been training racers and turning out successful career skiers this way for decades.

A few parents congregated near the lodge, waiting as their children approached. A couple of kids in the group headed back to the ski lifts to practice some more. That sort of persistence and drive would take them a long way.

And it drove his eyes back up the mountain to Terminator, which he couldn't see from here. Hudson's thoughts returned to the woman he'd tried to shove to the back of his mind all morning. Shannon's broken leg had healed just fine, but her knee continued to bother her, even after multiple surgeries. Even after the pain and trials of rehab.

Though she tried to hide it, he could tell. With today's technology, which was much improved from even ten years ago, the prognosis was good for a skier to return to the slopes again after a massive blow to the knee.

But sometimes...*sometimes*...the injury wouldn't heal right no matter how much surgery or how many months, or years, of rehabilitation.

Sometimes, the knee simply wouldn't cooperate. Like Shannon's. Maybe she could learn to compensate for that in other ways, but it was as much a mental struggle as it was physical.

Hudson hoped and prayed that wasn't the case for Shannon. He couldn't stand to see her lose her dream after what he'd seen her go through. Her pain would be his pain.

She was impatient, and that could hurt her in the end.

Shannon didn't want to follow the ski progression that had been outlined for her: take it slow. Tackle the easy runs at first. Then a few gates, and if that went well, progress through the steeper ski runs. Hudson understood all too well her impatience—if she followed the progression as outlined, she wouldn't be back in the game by next season.

She'd lose her momentum.

Then it could be over for her. She might never make world-class status or even come close to realizing her dreams—and Hudson had his own experience with that. On the other hand, she could make a big comeback if she were patient.

But the biggest risk of all? If she pushed herself too hard and too soon, she could injure herself permanently.

Any way he looked at it, it was a risk. The price was high. Too high, if you asked him, but apparently she didn't value his opinion.

Hudson headed to the T-Chair—the lift that would take him to the summit for Terminator. Maybe she'd already come down and he'd missed her, or maybe she was still up there, but Hudson needed a challenge of his own to clear his mind, give him clarity.

The decision he needed to make couldn't be ignored any longer.

He slid into the chairlift and rode up alone. This way he could watch the mountainside. Look for Shannon. She'd been his student for the past four years, starting when he'd come to Ridgewood as an assistant coach at only twenty-six years old, four years after his own alpine skiing career had come to a catastrophic end.

And that was why he had to make this decision. He cared deeply about what happened to her, like he cared about all his students.

He scraped his hand through his hair, silently repeating those words.

The time he'd spent helping her through rehabilitation, encouraging her and pulling her out of her manic state of mind, had created an emotional connection between them that he couldn't ignore. But it was one-sided at best.

He couldn't, shouldn't, feel this way about her. She was his student. She trusted him as her coach. He'd seen firsthand what a romantic relationship between a coach and a team member could do to the morale of the entire team. The reasons tallied up, but even if none of those stood between them, he couldn't let himself love. He didn't deserve it, after what he'd done.

The ski lift approached the drop-off and Hudson waited for it, then slid forward and out of the chair. With his poles, he shoved out of the way for the next chair coming up behind him, and he headed to the far side of the run to get a look at the skiers.

Shannon wasn't among those standing around, but it was a big mountain. For a second, Hudson considered skiing outside the resort boundaries—there, he'd be alone with the mountain and God.

What was he thinking to even consider it? That would be too risky, and he'd ended his life of reckless skiing years ago. Nothing could drive him out of bounds now.

He surveyed the challenging ski run below him and the surrounding view. No matter how many times he'd been up the mountain, been awed by its majesty—the clear blue sky and fresh snow of a bluebird day—he'd never get tired of it.

Positioning himself at the top of the slope, Hudson pulled in a breath, then shoved off. Momentum caught him quickly on the steep hill, and he tried to enjoy the feel of the mountain as he focused on the 45 percent grade and sharp turns. He couldn't afford to think about anything else, and yet Shannon edged into his thoughts.

Shoulders square to the fall line, he picked up speed

and tucked—squatting forward, ski poles positioned under his arms.

Focus or die.

A fall at this speed could do significant damage. The thought turned his mind to Shannon again and the race in which she'd crashed.

He knew he'd never get over the accident that had hurt his sister, Jen, and coaching others was supposed to help him right a wrong. But after watching Shannon take that fall, and the panic that had ensued inside him, Hudson knew he should admit what he'd known at that moment— he couldn't do this anymore.

Maybe he shouldn't even be coaching alpine ski racers, and that was the crux. Young and rising ski racers were depending on him to deliver his best.

The slope drove him down, harder and faster. Thirty minutes later, Hudson neared the end of the run, and thankfully, he'd gained a measure of control over his unbridled thoughts. He spotted the familiar turquoise ski suit. Could be someone else, but the woman tugged off the helmet and goggles and shook out her long, auburn tresses.

Shannon.

Relief blew over him to see her standing uninjured. He skied toward her, insides tensing.

He wasn't looking forward to the conversation he was about to have with her.

Chapter 2

Piper, one of Shannon's Ridgewood teammates, stopped just short of Shannon and tugged off her helmet.

"Great job, Shannon! You looked good up there."

At twenty, Piper was only a couple of years younger than Shannon, and she was already making inroads into the ski-racing world. Shannon was slightly jealous, but she beamed at the compliment. She didn't hear anything but sincerity from her companion, or rather, her competition.

"I didn't realize you were ready for that yet." The clouds had finally moved out, and Piper squinted in the sun. "You're glowing, though. Had to feel good to get back to the challenging stuff. How's the knee?"

Shannon wasn't sure if Piper really wanted to know or if she was trying to remind Shannon of her limitations. "It's as good as new."

Not too bad.

So her knee had plagued her a little. Shannon had been injured before, and with more hard work, she would make a comeback. She wouldn't be the first to go through this. She wouldn't be the last.

Piper quickly forgot Shannon and struck up a conversation with a cute guy Shannon didn't know, leaving her to her thoughts.

After months laid up so her leg could heal and a few surgeries to repair her knee, plus incessant therapy and retraining, it felt good to tackle Terminator.

Exhilarating, actually.

Shannon gulped in a breath and shoved her hair up into a ponytail. She'd needed to feel that again. The confidence it brought. She wasn't done skiing, and her dream wasn't over by a long shot, no matter the doubts she'd seen behind Hudson's eyes. Yes, shoving aside his warnings had bothered her, but now she'd proven his fears misplaced.

Though some ice on her knee might be a good idea.

Glancing up the slopes, she spotted the man himself. She'd hoped to avoid him for now. But he skied toward her with purpose. She scrunched up her nose. He hadn't followed her down, had he?

She wouldn't doubt it. He was persistent when it came to coaching. She'd always admired that about him, and she knew that was what had helped her to become a success. But…she could do with less of his diligence at the moment. They weren't seeing eye to eye.

"I think I'll head back up." Piper eyed the ski lift. "You want to come?"

How she wanted to. "No." Shannon eased onto the bench to remove her skis. "I need to grab lunch, and then I'm scheduled to work."

Fearing she might see a smirk, Shannon didn't look at Piper.

"I hope Hudson saw you ski that. It was awesome." Piper shoved off in the direction of the lift. "See you later, Shannon!"

"Yeah, later," she called. In her peripheral vision, she saw Hudson moving in her direction. He had a ways to go to reach her.

Maybe she could escape, get lost in the Thursday ski crowd before he caught her. She wanted a few moments to savor what she'd accomplished before he reprimanded her.

Shannon noticed a little girl, not more than six years old, standing a few yards away. Her skis went right out from under her, leaving her in an awkward position.

Still in her ski boots, Shannon jumped up and clomped over to assist her. "Oh, sweetie. Let me help you." Shannon grabbed her by the waist and helped her back up, holding her in place and keeping her steady. "Where's your mommy and daddy?"

"Over there."

Shannon glanced in the direction the girl pointed to see a man assisting a woman with her boots and skis. She laughed to herself. "Why don't you and I just hang here for a few minutes until your daddy can get your mommy ready? Are you taking one of the classes?"

The girl shook her head, curls bursting out of her bright pink helmet. "Uh-uh. Daddy says he can teach us."

Pursing her lips into a smile, Shannon thought about how many times that did *not* work out. Living and working at a ski resort, she'd seen it firsthand plenty of times. The girl's father finally glanced over at her, his face a little sheepish when he saw Shannon standing by his daughter and watching him. He left his wife, still unsteady herself, and skied over.

"She fell over. I helped her up." She hadn't meant that to sound as if she wanted to be a hero. "Why don't you put her in a class? She'd love it, and that would give you some time to teach your wife."

"I can handle it," he said, "but thanks for your help."

Shannon shrugged and returned to the bench for her

skis. In the distance, she watched the man struggle with his wife and daughter. Some people were just too stubborn for their own good. He'd probably end up the most frustrated of the three.

Positioning her skis over her shoulder, she stomped around the deck and entered the lodge that her father owned and ran. The lodge where Shannon had lived most of her life with her father. After storing her skis, she removed her ski boots and slipped into her shoes. She tugged off the top of her ski bib, letting it hang down.

She had to work at the lodge this afternoon, so she needed to grab a quick lunch. Working part-time, training— or retraining—to race and working on her online business degree didn't leave much time for a social life. But living at a resort made that pretty much an all-inclusive package.

Shannon shoved through the great room crowded with skiers—men, women and children of all ages donned in brightly colored skiwear and Nordic sweaters. Thursday began the long ski weekend, and the crowds thickened considerably compared to the rest of the week.

Between the lodge, the ski lift tickets and the restaurant, Daddy made a killing. The rustic, varnished pine of the great room boasted forty-plus square feet, and an entire wall of windows accented the rock fireplace. No wonder so many flocked to the room during the evening, after ski hours.

Acting as if she was just another patron, Shannon headed across the room to the Rusty Nail Café, which served as the only place to grab decent grub for a few miles. The crowd was big today, and the line was long. Shannon would need to push her way through to the kitchen, where a plate of chicken fingers and fries awaited her. Being the daughter of the ski-lodge owner had its advantages, but she expected to receive a few glares even though she would apologize profusely. Happened every time.

"Shannon."

Jack.

The familiar, unwelcome voice knocked around inside her.

She paused, hesitating, not wanting to face him, but she couldn't simply ignore him. Plastering on her best smile, she turned to face her ex-boyfriend.

"Hey, stranger, what are you doing here?" she asked.

He'd been invited to train with a world-class coach in a different country, had earned a spot on the U.S. Development Team and had pretty much been making tracks in the ski world while Shannon suffered through surgeries and rehab.

While she curled into a ball on her bed, tears and depression keeping her immobile because she couldn't ski. She realized just how much her life, her whole identity, was wrapped up in downhill racing, and if she couldn't get back to the place she was before, she didn't know what she'd do. Who she was.

Jack studied her now, his presence a painful reminder of all she'd lost with that one fall.

Shannon was glad for his successes and grateful she was over him on a personal level.

"I have some news. Wanted you to hear it from me first."

And now he had news... *How thoughtful.*

That he'd just pushed her aside and kept going with his career as if she'd meant nothing to him had hurt. On the other hand, what did she expect him to do? If she cared about him, she would have wanted him to go on without her, right?

But maybe if he had looked back for even a moment, acted as if he had been as devastated as she had been, even at the smallest level, she could have been comforted by that.

And now she didn't know why it should make a difference. They weren't an item anymore. He'd taken up with someone else. Someone on the road to a promising career.

Just remember, Jack, you're only one crash away from losing it all.

"News?" Shannon loathed the revealing swallow that followed her question. "What news?"

"I'm headed to Copper Mountain."

Copper Mountain. That constriction in her throat again. "You mean…"

"Well, to Vail first, where they'll announce the U.S. Ski Team."

"Oh, Jack." Shannon stepped forward and hugged her friend. They were friends before anything else, weren't they? "I'm so happy for you."

And she was.

He pulled away and looked at her. "Are you?"

His grin revealed his pleasure in his accomplishment, and his question would suggest he was concerned for her.

"Of course! Why wouldn't I be?"

"It's just that…" He trailed off.

She saw in his eyes that he expected her to be jealous. *Wanted* her to be jealous. And unfortunately, that very uncharitable emotion seemed to flood her being. But it also infused her with determination to succeed.

"You've worked hard for it," she reassured him. "I don't know anyone who deserves it more than you."

He took her hands and lifted them to his lips, planting a tender kiss on them both. "I'm so relieved to hear you say that."

His touch was unexpected and unwanted. Shannon tried to slip her hands free without revealing how uncomfortable she was. "So, you'll be at Copper Mountain, then."

A little less snow than Vail made it perfect for training.

"What does…um…Emily think about all this?" Emily,

the new girl in his life, who hadn't fallen, injuring herself right out of the limelight.

"She's thrilled. Very supportive."

Shannon didn't want to know if Emily would be staying in Copper Mountain with him as he trained. She didn't want to know anything. "Well, it's great to see you, and congratulations again. I'm going to be late if I don't get going."

Didn't he know there were more things in life? There had to be more, didn't there? But this…this was all Shannon wanted. All she knew.

"Oh, sure. I didn't mean to keep you," he said. "Glad I found you."

She caught herself before she asked how much longer he'd be in town. Leaving him standing there, she hurried past a family of five that had just arrived and were checking into the lodge.

"Good to see you, Jack." Hudson's voice rang through the lobby, strong and sure.

The man was a permanent fixture at the lodge since he'd come on board. When he wasn't coaching the members of the ski team, he volunteered at the adaptive ski program at another resort. He brought a whole new meaning to training, and though his philosophies sometimes conflicted with the ski-team board members', including her father's, the team had gained upward momentum under his training.

He cared about each member of the team on a personal level, and that fostered a real sense of camaraderie. Almost everyone called him by his first name instead of Coach Landers. And yet, he maintained a subtle distance, keeping the details of his own life to himself.

Behind a fake tree, she hung back and watched him congratulate Jack.

Jack's progress up the proverbial ladder of ski-racing success was in part due to Hudson's coaching. Seeing the two of them together, she remembered how after the accident Hudson had been there for her, really been there for her, even curbing his travel schedule with the team to help her through some rough spots.

His words to her the day she'd fallen swept through her thoughts now.

I'm right here, Shannon. I'm not going anywhere.

And he hadn't. Her heart warmed at the memory. He'd stayed by her side, helping her get back on her feet in every way. Hard to believe her ski coach had been a better friend than Jack, who'd whispered promises of love to her. Hudson had even been more attentive than Daddy, who was busy running the business that kept her on skis, but she knew she'd fallen a few notches in her father's eyes that day. He'd been counting on her, after all. His whole life, the lodge, centered on the abilities he'd seen in her at an early age before her mother had died.

But Hudson...*he* still believed in her. Didn't he?

At the moment, she could use someone to confide in, but she couldn't envision pouring all the ugliness, the jealousy and the pain out to her coach. He'd think she wanted to race again, compete again, for the wrong reasons.

With him, it was all about passion. All about the heart.

Behind the tree, she swiped at an errant tear. At least Jack had cured her from ever falling in love. She couldn't possibly go through that hurt again. Having someone love her only as long as she was a success.

And if she fell...more than her career was over.

Chapter 3

Hudson spent the afternoon in the lodge's mini conference room, reviewing videos of the team, discussing their strengths and weaknesses with the assistant coaches, even though they were short a coach until next week, when Jason would return from his Caribbean honeymoon.

Funny that a ski coach would choose the tropics. Hudson chuckled to himself. But maybe a change in scenery would do him some good.

This weekend they'd go over the strategies they discussed with the team members in preparation for the race in Telluride at the end of the month. The team raced against different ski clubs at the regional and divisional levels, and that was where a skier could really stand out, showing potential for even greater things. Hudson saw great promise in at least two team members. They needed everything he could give them, but there was a problem.

Something was missing for Hudson. Or rather, someone. Shannon was out of the competition for now.

He owed the ski team his best. She'd become a distraction, no doubt there.

But he owed her, too. This had started out to be her season. Her year. Did she blame him for her fall? Others had skied the same slope that day and not fallen. Accidents happened, he reminded himself, but that dismissive philosophy didn't appease him, especially regarding the downhill race with its dangerously high speeds.

Unfortunately during today's meeting, he'd been asked about Shannon's training schedule and when she would be back in the race. He didn't have an answer for that. Things became complicated at this juncture, and someone's life, their career and dreams rested in his hands. He'd let the other coaches know he would deal with Shannon.

And he would when he figured out how.

Stepping out of the conference room, he found the foyer empty, the great room quiet while everyone hit the slopes for one last run before supper. Shannon appeared engrossed in a magazine as she sat at the registration desk— her father's answer to her reduced training schedule while she healed, though she had to spend plenty of time in the gym. Hudson doubted she could take much more of sitting on the sidelines.

That much was obvious after today.

He'd talk to her about the double black diamond first, see how it went. Get the truth from her if he could. He'd seen her helping that little girl, and the image had warmed his heart then. It warmed his heart now, and it gave him an idea that weaved through his mind and took hold. He'd invite her to join him as a volunteer for the disabled-skiers program. It would be a small step for Shannon outside of her world.

Hudson smiled. This could be good for her. Now if he could only figure out how to bring her around to his way of thinking. Unfortunately, he'd have to convince her father as well, even though Shannon was twenty-two and capable of making her own decisions. He stumbled against a small garbage receptacle. Shannon looked up, her hazel-green eyes stirring when she saw him. He liked that a little too much.

"Hi," she said.

She'd caught him watching her, no less.

He cleared his throat. "Hi."

He'd known her long enough to recognize the hurt in her eyes. Seeing Jack today had put that there, and it was strong enough to overshadow any trepidation she might have about what Hudson would say to her.

And why wouldn't it? He'd watched her relationship with Jack grow into something more than friendship. He'd feared, too, for more than Shannon's career when he'd seen the fall. He'd seen it happen too many times. One person in a couple became more successful than the other and then there was fallout.

By all accounts, she seemed to be over Jack, but it wasn't Hudson's business, and he felt like a heel butting into her personal life, even if only in thought. "I saw you today."

Pink rose in her cheeks and she looked down. "I know."

Instead of harassing her for breaking her training schedule, he simply asked, "So, how'd it go?"

The tension around her mouth eased. Maybe she realized he wasn't going to berate her. She should know he wouldn't. That wasn't his way.

"It was good." Her face glowed, telling him what skiing that run had done for her. Boosted her confidence, exhilarated her.

He'd been the one who'd tried to stop her. He had his reasons.

The flicker of something amiss disappeared in the shadow of her gaze, telling him his reservations had been right. There was more to tell, but Shannon was keeping that to herself.

He had strong suspicions he already knew the problem. Except now wasn't the time for him to dig. She was working. But he wasn't sure he could wait.

He grinned, hoping she'd be more willing to open up. "I wish I could have seen it."

Except he'd told her not to go, something he'd need to address. He might have said more, but a couple approached the registration counter. Hudson could speak to Shannon tomorrow during her training session, except he wanted to know everything today.

"Will you be around later?" Though he cared about the members of his ski team as individuals—they worked hard and played hard together—he nevertheless maintained a safety net. An invisible line that protected everyone involved. Safe distance was important, especially with Shannon. That task grew more difficult with each day he spent with her. He and Shannon had known each other for four years now, spent plenty of evenings together in their travels to races.

But as a team.

Doubt niggled that he should wait until tomorrow to talk about Terminator, but he knew he'd lay awake wondering all night long.

Shannon eyed the approaching couple who held hands, enraptured with each other, then she glanced at him.

He understood why she'd disobeyed him. He got it—but she needed to understand where he was coming from. She stared at him—*now* he saw the wariness in her eyes. She had thought she could avoid this conversation today.

A chuckle escaped before he could catch it. He'd seen some of himself in her. "I want to hear the details. You know we have to talk." He sent her a wry grin. "That okay with you?"

Maybe other coaches wouldn't be so easygoing with her, but Hudson was worried about more than her health, or about whether or not she'd ever win another race, or about her gaining a shining career that reflected his skills as a coach.

Hudson was concerned about her as a person and what she was going through inside.

Smiling for the fast-approaching couple, she tucked her magazine under the counter. "Sure. Eight-thirty in the great room?"

Hudson nodded and stepped out of the way, making room for the new arrivals. Tonight he and Shannon would discuss what had happened on the slopes today, but the truth was he wanted to see her for a reason that had nothing to do with skiing.

He glanced at his watch. Five-thirty. Just enough time for a good long run around the suburban neighborhood where he lived. Santa Fe was about a half-hour drive, and he lived on the outskirts of town. Maybe the icy chill of the evening, with the record lows expected this week, would knock some cold sense into him.

Shannon crunched along the snow-packed sidewalk, heading away from the cabin her father had built for them five years ago when he'd wanted to move them out of the lodge. He needed a way to separate work from play, he'd said. Even so, Shannon didn't think a cabin that was less than a few hundred yards away from the ski resort he owned was far enough. Besides, he'd turned his play into his work. They were one and the same. No escape there.

Lights sprinkled around the lodge and parking lot, where couples walked hand in hand and families with young children headed home after a long day of skiing. Maybe they'd grabbed a bite at the Rusty Nail. A group of twentysomething men stashed their ski equipment in the back of an SUV. When there wasn't any vacancy at the lodge, skiers stayed at hotels between here and Santa Fe. Daddy had built up a thriving and successful ski resort, and she was proud of him. She wished she could return the favor—make him proud of her again.

Maybe Shannon could have moved to Minnesota and joined the infamous Buck Hill Ski Racing Team like other world-class athletes had done during their development years, or she could have gone to a ski academy or joined a college team. There were a lot of choices when it came to choosing a path that could take her as far as she wanted to go, but she'd chosen to stay close to home. Daddy wanted to build a lodge and resort that would accommodate and produce a leading alpine-racing team. Why send his daughter somewhere else? He'd built all this up for her— to make a way for her. And she knew, too, for him. This had been his dream before it ever belonged to her.

The thought gnawed at the back of her mind.

Nearing the lodge that resembled an enormous log-cabin palace, she was more than a little apprehensive about talking to Hudson tonight. He was always so offi-cial in some respects. Then in others, he was laid-back, like a best friend or someone you could confide in. He was young to be a head coach, but he had his own brand of training methods that had impressed the Ridgewood Ski Team Board. Daddy was the director and had hired him on as assistant coach. Two years ago, when head coach Tim Reeves had moved on, Hudson had been the natural choice to replace him.

But from the moment Hudson had joined Ridgewood, Shannon had struggled to think of him as her coach. When she was twelve, she had plastered her bedroom walls with action shots of him during the Olympics. She'd taken them down long ago, of course. When he'd first arrived, she'd walked around in a daze, in awe of him. But she'd had to let go of the schoolgirl infatuation. He was her coach and she was just a kid to him. Jack had come along and turned her head. At least there was something to be thankful about regarding that failed relationship.

Hudson wanted the members of the ski team to feel comfortable around him. She'd think that after knowing someone, working with them for that long, they couldn't help but be friends. But Hudson somehow managed to keep his distance.

He didn't *fraternize* with the ski-team members after hours. That was what made his request to meet with her this evening so unusual. After the stunt she'd pulled today, she had no idea what to expect from him, and his request just confirmed that.

Hands jammed in her pockets as she walked, she fidgeted. How possible was it for him to let her go from the team, when the resort belonged to Daddy? He was the director of the ski-team board. Would Hudson actually go that far?

For all she knew, he had the conference room reserved, setting her up to face off with all six coaches about today. At the thought, a vise squeezed her chest. Would they destroy the last shred of hope she held on to that she would race in competitions again in six months?

Though she wouldn't take their word for it until she'd seen Dr. Rollins for a follow-up, Hudson would have the final say. At least as far as the Ridgewood Team was concerned.

A few snowflakes landed softly on her cheeks. Shannon looked up to see the reflection of both the resort lights and the distant Santa Fe lights against the clouds, hanging weighty with their burden. Heavy snow was predicted, for which they could all be grateful. She hoped it would hold off until morning; that way she could hit the freshest powder on the mountain.

A chilly gust blasted over her. Tugging her parka tighter, she hurried the rest of the way until she reached the lodge. She pushed through a side door and moved down the hall that opened into the great room. Orange flames blazed in the oversize fireplace, and warm bodies wearing the latest fashion in ski sweaters filled every cushioned chair, sofa and ottoman, and the café tables on the dais. She couldn't hope to have a serious conversation with her coach here. All the more reason he'd probably usher her into the mini conference room.

Daddy stepped into her path, a smile covering the concern in his eyes. He gripped her shoulders. "I heard what you did today. Thought you'd be exhausted and go to bed early."

Shannon looked up at the handsome man in his midforties, only a little gray at his temples. He still turned heads, but he hadn't been interested in any woman since her mother, who had died when Shannon was young. He was a man who'd been a career skier himself until his life had taken a different direction, but the lodge kept him in the mix of things. She smiled. "I'm fine, Daddy. Everyone keeps trying to protect me, but I did the right thing. It was time."

His eyes lit up with approval as he nodded and tried to hide a yawn. "That's my girl."

"You know, maybe you're the one who needs to go home and rest." Her tone held a challenge.

He cocked his head. What could he say to that?

"You built us the cabin and yet you spend every minute here," she said. "Why should I be any different? I don't want to sit home alone."

He arched a brow. "As it happens, I was heading home just now when I saw you. Was just catching up with old friends who are staying to ski for a few days. Have anything against that?"

She tugged him to her and squeezed. "Of course not. I had to tease you."

"Honestly, I'd hoped you'd be around. Wanted to introduce you."

"Well? Where are they?"

"Already gone to bed. Sorry you couldn't meet them."

"Me, too."

"They'll be around tomorrow. You'll have your chance." Daddy tugged his cell phone out of his pocket.

While he peered at the buzzing phone, Shannon searched the crowd in the great room. Across the lobby, across the gathering of skiers sharing stories from their day, Shannon saw Hudson holding a mug and talking to a woman. A nice-looking, thirtyish woman. Maybe a little older than he.

When Shannon noticed that her father had put away his phone and followed her gaze, she realized she'd been staring at the cozy couple.

"I'll be home in a little while," she said. "I'm supposed to meet Hudson here."

Her father gave her a questioning look. A little twitch around his eye told her he recognized she might have crossed a line and pushed Hudson too far. "Let me know what he says about today."

He winked and strolled down the hallway to the side door where Shannon had entered. She started across the great room to Hudson. She'd heard him right, hadn't she? Tonight? Eight-thirty? As Shannon made her way, weaving through the people hanging out, she didn't see anything but the woman smiling up into his face—she was attracted to him. Interested in him. Shannon recognized that look, all right.

And why not? If anything, Hudson Landers was an attractive man. Strong and agile, he was an athlete second to his looks, and that was saying something.

Uncomfortable interrupting him while he was with the woman, Shannon stopped walking halfway across the room. She really didn't know much about Hudson's personal life—he'd kept things that way. When he had traveled with them to some of their races, he had never brought anyone with him. And he hadn't seemed in a hurry to get home to anyone, though she knew he wasn't married.

She decided to order a hot cocoa while she waited for Hudson to finish his business. Business that was already encroaching on her time. Had he forgotten he'd wanted her to meet him here?

In addition to the Rusty Nail Café, the lodge offered a full coffee bar. Shannon ordered her hot chocolate and chatted with the barista, a longtime friend.

Cecile handed the mug over the counter, shoving her short curly hair from her eyes. "Be careful. It's hot."

In her mid- to late thirties, Cecile had been at the lodge for as long as Shannon could remember, and she had been a good friend—probably the closest thing to a mother Shannon had had since Mom's death, except she was a little young for the job in both years and personality.

"Working late tonight, aren't you?" Shannon asked.

"I'm divorced. Where else am I gonna be?" She winked. "I get off in half an hour. Want to hang out?"

Shannon took a sip of her hot chocolate and peered over the rim across the great room. Hudson was still with that woman. Shannon shook her head. "I'm supposed to meet someone."

When she glanced back at Cecile, a slow grin spread across the woman's face. "Landers, huh?"

Why did Cecile have that look in her eyes? "He's my coach. You know that."

"Oh, excuse me—" she cleared her throat "—*Coach* Landers. You'd better go break up your coach and that woman if you plan on talking to him tonight." Cecile moved to another customer.

Maybe Cecile was right, although Shannon would prefer to forget the conversation she knew was coming. She'd brought it on herself.

But it had so been worth it. A little stiffness and pain wouldn't stop her.

Shannon edged her way across the room and closer to the fire. She'd always loved the way the flames danced in the evenings, creating the perfect ambience for good friends to share their stories. To kick back and relax. Her eyes drifted back to Hudson, who appeared pinned in by several couples on that side of the room. People relaxing before they went to bed so they could get up early and hit the mountain all over again—that is, if they weren't adventurous enough for a little night skiing.

Hudson Landers was Shannon's coach. He was what... thirty now? Just shy of a decade older than her, but it didn't seem like it the way they connected, especially during the toughest parts of her rehabilitation and training.

I'm right here, Shannon. I'm not going anywhere. To his credit, he'd definitely lived up to those words, but for how much longer?

For the first time in a very long time, well, since she'd ripped those posters from her wall, she looked at him. *Really* looked at him. She wanted to see what that woman saw.

He wore comfortable jeans and a crisp, warm navy sweater. One hand held the mug, the other was in his pocket. His hair was thick and dark, and though she couldn't see them from across the room, she knew his eyes to be a striking slate-blue—almost like the color of snow in the darkest shadows of the woods.

He'd been her hero when she was growing up. Hudson Landers, a rising Olympic star.

Hudson Landers wins the gold.

She could remember the headlines like it was yesterday. Then…nothing. He'd disappeared.

Hudson turned his head. From across the room, he stared at her. And Shannon had the alarming feeling that he'd known she was there, watching him the whole time. She had the urge to look away, but his gaze pinned her in place.

That connection again. He understood her.

Like no one else.

And she needed him to understand her now. Of all people, he should understand her need to race. Of all people, he would be the one to help her get back to the level at which she wanted to compete. It came to her just how much she counted on him. Too much. He held too much power over her.

With one word, he could make or break her career. With one word, he could destroy her hopes and dreams. She couldn't let that happen. She would show him, prove to him…

Shannon made a move toward him, and pain shot through her knee.

Chapter 4

"I'm anxious to hear your decision. I think this... Hudson?" Amanda Mason's voice edged into his mind.

He'd heard her, but his attention was riveted to Shannon as she made her way toward him.

Her eyes shined with an inner fire he recognized. A fire that was in danger of being snuffed out. Her smile, those amazing eyes and gorgeous hair weren't what held his attention as Amanda spoke to him. He'd seen Shannon's subtle favor to her right leg, the flicker of a grimace across her face.

Just as he'd suspected, her knee was bothering her. She was in pain. And far more than the deep ache of an injury that hadn't been given the chance to heal completely. She might not recognize it, but he did—the pain ran much deeper than physical.

While the ski run had exhilarated her, it might have done more harm than good. Inside, his own heart grimaced for what she was going through, and for the fact that he knew her much too well despite keeping his distance. He kept his smile in place and didn't let on that he'd read her. There was nothing he wanted to do more than rush to her side, and that revealed what a dangerous place he was in when it came to Shannon.

"Hudson?" This time, Amanda pressed her hand against his arm. "What's wrong?"

He swallowed, turning his attention back to yet another attractive woman. Beautiful and elegant. The creamy turtleneck hugged her neck, accenting her slender features. Her raven hair cascaded past her shoulders, and she tucked a few strands behind her ears, concern etching her forehead. He'd run into her while jogging earlier this evening, and the next thing he knew, she'd made plans to meet him at the lodge to talk about working with disabled skiers on a more permanent basis. Why couldn't he be interested in this woman? They even had a common interest. She knew what she wanted in life and who she was. The woman's identity wasn't wrapped up in herself.

For a million reasons, she was safer, but then again, no one was safe for him. Nor was it Amanda that drew his attention now.

"One of my students is headed this way," he said.

Amanda peered at Shannon around the circle of guys standing between them. "And you have a problem with that?"

Uh-oh. That was not what he meant. "Not at all. I told her to meet me here tonight."

"Would you like me to give you some privacy?" Amanda asked. Her vibrant smile went a long way to hide her disappointment should he say yes, but not far enough.

Amanda was the executive director of the disabled-skiers program at Ender's Peak Ski Resort. Every year, around two hundred volunteers from every walk of life assisted with the program, including Hudson. Amanda and the program director, Tom Carver, were the only full-time staff, but Tom planned to leave, hence Amanda's conversation with Hudson.

He'd gotten to know her a few weeks after he'd started volunteering with the program, and he enjoyed her company. He suspected she wanted a much closer friendship, but his main interest in her had everything to do with the disabled-skiers program. He didn't want to alienate her, but he didn't return her apparent attraction.

"I'd like you to meet her and then, yes, if you wouldn't mind, I need to talk to her alone as her coach. I have an issue that needs discussing, though maybe I didn't pick the right place to do that."

Considering that his thoughts turned to Shannon a bit too often, maybe he'd picked exactly the right place. Meeting with Shannon after hours and alone wasn't the right thing for him. For either of them. Maybe spending more time with Amanda was what he needed to do, after all, but the reasons wouldn't be fair to her.

"I won't be long. I promise," he added, but wasn't sure why he felt the need to explain.

When he pulled his gaze from Amanda, he spotted Shannon heading away from him instead of toward him like she had been.

"Looks like she changed her mind," Amanda said.

Without another word, Hudson pushed through the group of guys who were becoming boisterous, and moved to catch up with Shannon. He tried to act casual so he wouldn't draw unwanted attention to either of them, but he needed to get to her before she left. She disappeared down the side hall. By the time he got to the hallway, she had already pushed through the exit outside.

Unsure if he should follow her, Hudson paused in the hall and scratched his chin. Why had she left? Just because he'd been talking to Amanda? That didn't make any sense.

She wasn't his girlfriend. Neither was Amanda. Shannon had no reason to be jealous that he was talking to another woman. He'd told her he wanted to talk, and she knew he wanted to hear about the black diamond today. She knew he'd have a few words for her, but they were for her benefit.

Obviously, she used Amanda as an excuse to avoid him.

Regardless of her reasons for escaping, Hudson wanted her back in the lodge with the crowd. He no longer trusted himself. She might see something in his eyes that would give away his admiration, hint at something more, and he had to get a handle on whatever it was about Shannon that had slipped through his well-guarded defenses during her rehabilitation. The fall had devastated her, sending her into a deep depression, but she'd worked her way out of it. She'd trained hard, and he'd admired her inner strength. She deserved to race again and to win, if anyone did.

But what if that didn't happen?

Then what would she do? There was so much more to life, if only Hudson could make her see.

He shoved through the exit, cold air blasting his cheeks. He'd forgotten to grab his coat. A gust of wind stirred up flurries from a snowdrift, and they whipped around him. Laughter echoed nearby as a couple engaged in a snowball fight within the ring of lights around the lodge.

Fifteen feet ahead of him, Shannon marched away, her parka hood covering her head.

"Shannon!" he called and rushed forward. "Wait!"

She kept going. Hadn't she heard him? He took bigger strides to catch up. "Shannon."

She hesitated.

"Wait," he called. At that moment, he felt like anything but her coach.

She turned around, her eyes wide. "What are you doing?"

He closed the distance. "Me? What are *you* doing? We

were supposed to meet. To talk. You were walking straight toward me. What happened?"

She shrugged. "I thought I misunderstood when I saw you talking to your friend."

She *had* left because of Amanda.

"Amanda Mason." A laughing squeal filled his ears when a woman ran past. A snowball landed at his feet. He ignored the distraction. "I wanted to introduce you to her."

Shannon eyed the couple that had gotten a little too close in their game. She waited until they were out of earshot. "Why? Who is she?"

That hadn't been his initial intention when he'd agreed to meet Amanda at the lodge before Shannon, but now that he thought about it, introducing Shannon to Amanda was a good idea. Wishing he'd brought his coat, Hudson glanced back at the lodge. "Listen, can we talk back inside?" He grinned. "It's biting out here."

She frowned. "Can it wait? I'm tired. It's been a long day."

"That bad, huh?"

She angled her head. "What do you mean?"

"Your knee's bothering you." He thrust his hands into his pockets to keep them warm. "You figured you could hide it from me."

Shannon stood tall. "You're wrong on all counts. I'm fine to talk tonight, if it's that important."

"You don't need to be afraid." He grinned, hoping to bring a smile to her pensive gaze. "I'll go easy on you."

In truth, he wasn't so sure that Shannon shouldn't be concerned about their conversation. He wasn't sure he'd go easy on her. He didn't want to crush her dreams. And he wouldn't if he didn't have to, but he wasn't sure things would go that way this time. He hated that he thought about her the way he did. His emotions had to be clouding his judgment, but how did he stop them?

Hudson needed to maintain his professionalism. He had to make the right calls on this. More than his career was at stake. Shannon's dream was, too, and he didn't want that to be shattered like his own dreams were. He'd never completely recover from his personal loss, but if he could help someone else, prevent them from the complete physical and emotional devastation he'd experienced, then maybe that could make up for his mistakes.

Not likely. Not when his sister would never walk again. Not when she'd lost the love of her life on top of that.

But coaching alpine skiers with disabilities eased some of the pain. Teaching them how to adapt to the environment and ski like anyone else infused them with self-confidence, gave them freedom. Serving others had benefited him, as well. It had a way of taking a person's eyes off his own troubles. The Lord knew he needed to be free from his past, and maybe this would eventually take him there.

But he had another trouble a few feet in front of him. How did he deal with her? As Shannon forged ahead of him back to the lodge, he realized that he should be the one who was worried.

He had a feeling the next few moments, their conversation, would be a challenging course littered with obstacles.

Shannon tugged the heavy door open, but Hudson was the one to swing it all the way. He held it for her as she entered the warm lodge. She yanked off her jacket as she trekked down the hallway, aware that he trailed her, more than determined to have this conversation.

Her greatest fear pressed in on her. Hudson might not say what she wanted to hear. That he had an intuitive gift to know when she was hurting didn't help.

A hint of his musky cologne wafted over her when he drew up beside her in the hall. Together, they entered the great room. The crowd had diminished significantly as the evening grew late. Shannon paused, unsure where Hudson wanted to talk. But at least she wouldn't face six coaches in the mini conference room. Looked as if this would be a Coach Landers special-edition speech.

Placing his hand on her elbow, he gestured to the dais and a small table in the corner. "That should give us some privacy."

"Okay." Shannon's legs grew heavy with dread as they carried her across the hardwood floors and Nordic rugs.

Only about four inches taller than she, Hudson looked down and gave the same wicked grin he had sported in the posters that had sent her head spinning as a young girl. *Not that again.*

"Would you like something to drink?" he asked.

"No, thanks." *Let's just get this over with.* She couldn't take this anymore.

"Are you sure?" He paused and hung his thumbs on the pockets of his jeans. "I'm getting hot chocolate. Chasing you outside left me cold."

The grin again.

She shook her head. "You go ahead. I had some already."

"You're not going to run out on me again, are you?"

She could tell he was trying to lighten her mood. "I'll wait for you. I promise."

He ushered her the rest of the way to a table where his jacket was slung over a chair. "Glad to see my coat is still here. I'll be right back."

Hudson left her, and she sat with her back to the corner wall. Would Amanda join them, or had she left already? Seeing him with Amanda had made Shannon a little jealous, which was ridiculous.

A few moments later, Shannon watched Cecile hand two mugs to Hudson over the counter of the coffee bar. He turned and looked at Shannon as if he was checking on her. Seeing if she'd waited for him or if she had made another run for it. His hands bearing the mugs, he made his way back and slid into the seat across from her, then pushed the extra steaming cup over. "Just in case you get thirsty or cold or both."

"Thanks. That was thoughtful of you." Shannon wrapped her hands around the cup, enjoying its warmth. She'd never been with Hudson under these circumstances. Sitting at a table at the lodge while drinking a cup of hot chocolate. Alone. Maybe it wouldn't be such a big deal if she didn't still harbor a small crush on him. She thought she'd let go of that a long time ago, but here it was, resurfacing at the worst possible moment.

She'd be mortified if she let that slip. What did it matter? He was about to roast her over coals hot enough to melt the snow from beneath her dreams—in his own caring way.

Her whole identity was on the line here.

Shannon sipped the hot liquid, closed her eyes and drew in a long, slow breath, hoping he didn't notice how tense she'd become. When she opened her eyes, he stared at her.

He leaned back in the chair and studied her for longer than was comfortable. "You skied Terminator today after I gave you explicit instructions to stay away from that for now."

Great conversation opener. "Yes."

"So, talk to me."

Her throat constricted. That was it? "I'm sorry." But she wasn't. Not really.

"I'm not here to berate you, Shannon."

"Then what?" Her pulse raced. Was he going to let her go from the team? They'd known each other for so long. He'd been her hero.

"Relax, will you?"

Shannon blinked, hoping he didn't see the salty moisture threatening to surge in her eyes. She drew in a calming breath.

"I want to hear about your day. How you did on the run. More important, I want to hear how you're doing on the inside. Then when you're finished, I want to hear about your knee."

His incredible eyes had turned darker than usual. She couldn't hold his gaze any longer and stared at her remaining hot chocolate. He was back to the things of the heart again. He was a great coach, and she wouldn't have gotten this far without him, but for him it wasn't about winning. Daddy had hired the wrong guy.

Hudson and Shannon were diametrically opposed. If he could sense that she was in pain in spite of her efforts to hide it, she had a gift for sensing that now was the moment when she had to convince him that winning was everything.

But Shannon shoved those thoughts aside. She couldn't hope to convince him with so much weighing on her. She smiled instead. She let the highlights of her day infuse her heart, knowing Hudson would see that.

He would feel it.

"The mountain, the sky, the hill and the speed…it was glorious…." She let her words trail off.

If it was all about what mattered most in life, about things of the heart…let him see hers.

Hudson locked eyes with her, his gaze reflecting the wonder of the passion they shared. The fire in his eyes suffused her with hope that she wasn't a lost cause. That he believed in her, just like she'd always thought he had, and he would continue to believe in her. That Shannon could compete again and secure some wins. Daddy would be proud of her again, and so would Hudson. Jack would wish he hadn't so easily given her up.

Encouraged, she continued pouring out the experience,

describing every twist and turn of the run. How she felt more in control than she had in a long time. Except for the one thorn behind her kneecap, but she kept that part to herself.

"And when I reached the end, all I could think was that I'm back." *Oh, God, please let me be back. Let me convince him.*

When she dared to glance at Hudson's face again, she could tell he was hooked on her dream. Addicted to racing, just as she was. She didn't understand why he'd ever quit competitive skiing. He'd never shared the reason. Desperation compelled her, a boldness swept over her, and she reached across the table, placing her hand over his. Crossing an invisible line.

"I want to race again. You know this, and now is the time I need to push hard and fast."

He didn't edge away, or slip his hand from beneath hers, but kept it there, and an awkward and yet oddly comfortable moment settled between them. At the edge of his sweater collar, she could see the steady beat of the pulse in his neck. She'd love to know what he was thinking.

"I *have* to race again," she said. *It's all I know.* "I live and breathe to compete. Surely you of all people can understand that."

From across the small round table, he searched her eyes.

"Your knee?" he finally asked.

"I don't care about the risks."

He pulled away from her then, sliding his hand from beneath hers. The way his jaw worked, she knew he was anything but happy.

"You don't know what you're saying. Winning isn't everything." His voice was low and steady, carrying the weight of the world. "Life is more than a series of competitions. Why do you have to race?"

Why exactly, she wasn't even sure she knew. Maybe

because it had been instilled in her from a very young age. But should the man be coaching her if he wasn't here to help her win? The thought made her nauseous. She credited his training with her success before the fall. She wished everything could just go back to the way it was before that day.

"Hey, Hudson. Hey, Shannon." Rodney, another team member, leaned against their table, interrupting them. "Funny seeing you here."

It might look like more than it was to Rodney, and that wouldn't go over well with the rest of the team or coaches, Shannon knew, especially if Rodney had witnessed her hand covering Hudson's.

"Just telling our coach about skiing Terminator today."

"You did?" Rodney's eyes widened in delight.

"Yep. And I lived to tell about it. But he's all yours now." Shannon slid from the chair and used the interruption to escape.

Rodney eagerly took Shannon's place, and she left Hudson to work his jaw.

Chapter 5

Shannon shifted beneath the lavender sheets, then opened her eyes. Early-morning light beamed through the crack in the matching curtains with a bright force that could mean only one thing. She eased from the bed and tugged the window treatments open. The harsh white of fresh powder reflected back, and the stillness that always accompanied new snow framed the forest with an awe-inspiring, postcard-worthy splendor.

Her heart jumped at the sight, but her unfinished conversation with Hudson tempered her delight. The tenor of the exchange had stayed with her, hovering at the edge of her dreams throughout the night, leaving her with an unsettled feeling that clung to her this morning.

The beauty and promise of a great day on the ski runs would go a long way toward helping her bury their conversation. At least for the moment. Shannon considered heading up to Mountain King, one of her favorite hills and where they often trained, for a quick, invigorating run down the slope. That was, before it was time to train, before too many people sloshed across the slope and ruined the powder.

If the snow was too wet, Hudson and the others would salt the course to make it hard and even for training.

Training. She sighed.

Was that what he had planned to tell her last night? That she wasn't ready to seriously train with the team yet, that she would be relegated to the easy runs even though she'd completed the double black diamond? His last words to her had sure made it sound that way.

As she leaned against the window and stared out, her heavy sigh created a circle of fog against the glass. It was as if the whole world weighed on her shoulders—everyone was disappointed in her. No matter which way she turned, what choices she made, someone would be let down. Maybe even God, but He'd let her down, too. She'd spent her whole life working toward this one goal. How could He let her fall? Let this happen?

She couldn't help but consider that Hudson might be relieved if she just quit racing for good. Was that what he really wanted? The man who believed that the passion of skiing and racing had to stem from the heart. That it couldn't be taught.

No.

He'd been the one to pull her out of her depressive funk and talk her through it, getting her mind back on recovering. He'd even told her that down the road she'd see it was only a blip in her career. But all the practice and persistence and patience in the world didn't guarantee she'd return. She knew that as well as he did, but he'd never said it then. Last night she'd heard something much different in his tone.

Another voice whispered to Shannon. If she didn't race and win, no one would be there for her, not even Hudson, despite his words. That was already evident when Jack dumped her so quickly. And her father had put everything into this—this had been his dream, and somehow he'd made her believe it was hers.

But no matter whose dream it started out to be, it was hers now. Without skiing, without racing in competitions, who was Shannon?

She didn't know.

But what she *did* know was that she had every intention of training today. Let Hudson tell her otherwise. What did she have to lose if he planned to completely dismiss her from the team, anyway? This could be her last chance to prove to him she was ready.

After getting dressed for the slopes, she headed to the kitchen and prepared coffee while she waited on her microwave oatmeal.

Her father emerged from the hallway and squeezed her shoulder. "So what did Landers have to say?"

Shannon drew in a long, hot swallow of the vanilla-laced coffee. She was trying her best to forget how things had ended. "I'm headed out to the slopes to train with the team. Can we talk about this later?"

Her father raised his brows. "You're training with the team again? That's good news, but what did he have to say about skiing Terminator?"

Hudson might technically work for her father and the Ridgewood Ski Team Board, but her father gave him control and leeway in his decisions regarding ski-team members, including Shannon. That might prove to be volatile over the next few days or weeks. She hated to see what would happen should her coach dismiss her for what she'd pulled yesterday. Though she didn't believe he would, Daddy was obviously watching closely. He'd been proud when Hudson had come aboard and the team had made a few headlines. Everything went smoothly as long as Shannon was the star, but her insides tensed as she pictured herself being pulled in opposite directions by the two most important men in her life.

Shannon turned her back to finish assembling her breakfast. "We were interrupted. Didn't finish the conversation."

"This next season is going to be your season. You just watch. Glad he finally gave you the go-ahead."

"I didn't say he did. I said I was headed to the slopes to train with them. I'm hoping to convince him that I'm ready." She faced him again and stirred her steaming bowl of blueberry-topped oatmeal.

Her father gave her a thoughtful look. "Tread carefully, Shannon. You might push the man too far. You need to be a good example for the rest of the team. For now, at least. Next season, we'll make the move for you to start stepping out on your own more often. But you don't want to rush yourself. Listen to Landers. He knows what he's doing. That's why I hired him."

She cringed inside. Her father was always full of encouragement, but he was sidestepping the truth. He and Hudson hadn't agreed on much in a long time, especially when it came to winning. Daddy believed in racing to win, and he didn't tolerate quitters.

He used to micromanage her career, but that didn't work for either of them, so he'd kept his distance, giving the reins to the ski-team coaches. It sounded as if he was gearing up to micromanage again, which was difficult considering his focus was split between her ski-racing career, the team and running the resort and lodge.

When she didn't answer, he continued, "I have complete confidence in him. Even though our philosophies clash on some points, Ridgewood has done well under his training."

"Okay, Daddy." Shannon hoped that would be the end of it.

He chuckled. "That's my cue to leave."

Her father grabbed his coffee and headed back to take a shower and prepare for the day.

Shannon guzzled her cooled-down coffee, feeling it churn in her stomach. Plenty of girls her age were on the full-time skiing circuit and had been for years. Shannon had hoped to be there six months ago before she took that debilitating, life-altering fall. Her father had been equally disappointed, if not more so. Hudson had been further along in his career than she was when he was her age—she'd had the posters to prove it.

But everyone was different. Some hit the scene in a big way later. Then some were taken out completely by an injury.

Somehow, she had to keep that from happening. She hoped it went well on the slopes today. Shannon downed her coffee and made another cup. Hudson's training sched-ule for her didn't include the drills he had set up for the team at large. Surely he wouldn't hold her back any longer. She missed being involved with the team, missed the camaraderie.

After gulping down her oatmeal, Shannon found her father and kissed him on the cheek. "Have to go now."

"I'm headed to Santa Fe this afternoon for supplies and groceries. Want to come?"

"Ask me later today."

Shannon finished assembling her gear and, at the door, put on her ski boots. That was the most awesome part of living at a resort—she could walk out her front door and catch a ski lift up the mountain.

Positioning the skis over her shoulder, she left the cabin. Then she headed for the lift that would take her to Mountain King, where she hoped to find the team gathering.

Normally, she spent the first two hours in the gym, then skied according to the training schedule—and that was the problem. The program wasn't the challenge and speed she was accustomed to in the past, and she was itching for more.

She ignored the dread stirring inside her at Hudson's possible reaction to her appearance today. Outside, Shannon hiked to the end of the sidewalk connected to the cabin that she shared with her father. The lodge stood three hundred yards away, and she spotted Cecile locking her car in the parking lot. Must have the morning shift. The woman headed to the lodge and glanced Shannon's way. Seeing her through the trees, Cecile tossed her a wave. Shannon lifted her hand in acknowledgment.

Turning toward the mountain, she stepped into snow that was almost thigh high in places. On days like this when she had to raise her knees and march through the thick powder, she imagined it was moondust and she wore a space suit, especially with the heavy ski boots. By the time she made it to her destination, she'd have a decent workout for most people.

The Mountain King chairlift came into view on the other side of a grove of snow-packed evergreens, where her coach stood with several of the team members. For those still in school, their schedules usually allowed them flexibility, but this week they had off anyway. The others were already riding up in the chairs, on their way to the top of the ski run. Her pulse ratcheted up. She'd already pushed it with him. If skiing Terminator hadn't been enough, showing up to train with the team today might be too much. What was she doing? It was as if someone had opened the gate and once she'd taken off, she couldn't stop—she was ready for more. Couldn't he see that?

Panicked, Shannon ducked behind a tree along the wooded trail, hoping that would keep him from seeing her. Joining the team when they were already engaged on the slope would be best. Approaching them now would give Hudson too much opportunity to turn her away if that was his intention. Her manipulative tactics weighed on her, but not enough to stop her.

While she waited, she spotted the blue salt bags hanging out of the garbage. Daddy would make sure someone saw to that soon. The coaches had already prepped the slope for training earlier this morning and for all she knew distributed gates for slalom skiing.

Rodney's laughter drifted all the way to her where she hid. He was the comedian of the group, and even if no one else thought his jokes were funny, his laughter was contagious. Maybe that would keep Hudson's attention long enough. Hopefully, Rodney hadn't gotten the wrong idea when he'd seen her and their coach together last night.

At the thought, Shannon remembered that moment—she'd been desperate and bold and had simply reached out to make him understand the only way she knew how. But the way he'd kept his hand in place beneath hers for so long, she could almost imagine something more had passed between them. That thinking was wrong and crazy.

She shoved her silly romantic thoughts away. That was not where her focus should be. At the top of Mountain King, she couldn't reach out to Hudson like that today if he didn't react to seeing her like she hoped he would. But she didn't think he would be too harsh—what would that do for everyone's morale if they thought a severe injury meant getting tossed from the team eventually? That was the wrong message, and it wasn't his way.

She loved that about him. If anything, he'd use her devastating fall to impress upon everyone the importance of training, safety and following the rules.

Never mind she was bending a few of those today, but

she'd done everything he said back in November, and she'd still been injured anyway.

"Shannon!"

She lifted her gaze to see Cecile making her way over from the lodge.

Shannon swatted at her and then held a finger to her lips.

Cecile frowned and trudged forward, hugging herself even though she wore her bright orange ski jacket. She was breathing hard by the time she reached Shannon.

"Why are you hiding behind a tree?" Cecile asked.

"If you knew I was hiding, why did you call my name? Why did you walk toward me?" Shannon quirked a brow.

Cecile laughed. "Don't worry. They're gone. Everyone is on the ski lift, riding up."

Shannon peered from behind the tree to confirm what her friend had said. "Oh, good. I thought you'd blown my cover."

"I was going to ask how it went with Mr. Coach last night, but now I'd rather know why you're hiding from him." She held a mischievous grin. The way she acted made her seem much younger than her mid-thirties.

"I have to run." Shannon headed to the ski lift.

"You're going up? Are you sure that's a good idea?"

"I'll tell you everything tonight. Wouldn't you rather hear the whole story, including the end?"

"Be careful up there," Cecile called.

Waving at the lift operator, Shannon grabbed the next chair, thankful it was six seats behind the team. Behind Hudson. The chairs between them were empty because the lifts weren't open to the public for another hour, but he likely wouldn't glance behind him. She watched him laughing at Rodney's animated story. Her heart warmed, and some of her trepidation subsided. Hudson wanted what was best for her, she told herself.

Making an entrance like this hadn't exactly been her plan. Now she wished she'd stayed and finished her conversation with him last night. She could hardly stand to think about the way he'd looked at her when she left, the challenge in his last words.

Today…no more words. Only action.

The lift finally approached the launch point, and Shannon's pulse raced as if she was at the starting gate. When the chair reached the top, just before it wound around to head back down, she shoved forward and used the momentum to skate over to the team. Just a few yards away, everyone hung around Hudson.

On his every word.

"…hips in play, shoulders level, shins parallel. If you're patient, you'll find the fall line and that's key. But more important than any of that is to enjoy the day. I want to see smiles out here. If you're not having fun—" he paused when he spotted Shannon "—then what's the point?"

The familiar words wrapped around her even as everyone's attention drifted from their venerated coach over to her. After he finished his spiel, he joined the others as they stared at her—and the silence nearly killed her. But even worse, something she couldn't read burned behind his eyes.

She'd made a mistake. Shannon wished she could fall into a crevasse.

Was she really going to challenge him in front of the team?

Lord, what do I do with this girl? They hadn't finished their conversation last night, and maybe she'd misunderstood, but he doubted that was the case. Maybe he was being too hard on her.

"Again, I want to reiterate how important it is to be patient. Don't rush yourself." Though he said the words to the group of young athletes, they were meant for Shannon.

He smiled to ease the tension he saw in her face. His last words to her had been a little harsh, stemming from his own issues: *Life is more than a series of competitions. Why do you have to race?* He was beginning to question his coaching abilities, especially when it came to Shannon. "It's great to see you on the slope with us today."

"I'm glad to be here," she said. With his words, shining enthusiasm quickly replaced the apprehension in her gaze. "I've missed training with the team."

An overwhelming outburst of "welcome backs" erupted from the small huddle. Clearly, they'd missed their star team member. Maybe he'd been wrong to keep her training on her own for so long, but he feared her competitive spirit would drive her to push harder and faster than she was ready for. Apparently that hadn't made a difference, considering yesterday's run on the double black diamond.

The girl was driven—just like Hudson had been years ago. Why had he believed that she would listen to him at this juncture of her retraining? She'd been holding back for so long, and he understood that.

At seeing her enthusiasm, his heart jumped. Thank goodness he was able to hide his admiration from the others. A coach showing favoritism was never a good thing. Discovering that his esteem for her sprang from something much more would be a disaster. At least they all admired Shannon, and with good reason.

Hudson refocused his attention on the team. Reining in their wholehearted welcomes, he finished his instructions. Then when the students lined up to take their turn at the slope, he gestured Shannon over and out of earshot.

"Showing up here was a little presumptuous, don't you think?" He watched Rodney take off down the slope.

"Thank you." Her gaze jumped to the ground at her feet.

Not the response he expected. "For what?"

"For not laying into me in front of the team."

"You know better than that. I'd never do that to you. Or anyone. I have something else in mind for you."

She stiffened. "What?"

He yanked back the teasing grin itching to get out. "Don't worry, I don't have any intention of scolding you." *Just yet.*

"Then what?" Shannon shifted her weight off her knee.

Was that for a reason? Or was he reading more into it than a simple redistribution of weight.

"We didn't finish our conversation last night." Hudson dug his ski poles into the snow. "Though I'm not convinced this is the right thing yet, let's see how you do today. But on one condition."

Shannon's shoulders inched down. "What's that?"

"I'll call Dr. Rollins and schedule you to get your knee examined again on Monday."

"Ahead of the follow-up in two weeks?" She shrugged. "Fair enough."

Hudson smiled. Maybe he was overreacting. If only he had someone he could talk to about this. He wasn't sure he was seeing the situation clearly. There were plenty of better coaches with decades more experience than he had. But did any of them struggle the same way he struggled? Did any of them carry the weight of a devastating past around with them like he did? He never thought that the past would creep into his decision making like this.

"Everything okay?" Shannon's question pulled him back.

Of course, he hadn't forgotten she stood there waiting for his instructions. The way she looked at him now, though, he knew she'd seen past his smile. "Nothing you need to worry about."

Hudson dived right into what he wanted from her today. "No pushing it, okay? In fact, you might want to take the day off, since you skied Terminator yesterday, just to be safe."

"I'm good." Her eyes were bright. "Really."

"Take your time through the middle corridor. Throw your hands forward if you think you're in trouble. Adapt."

She nodded. "Got it." And pulled her goggles over her eyes. The rest of the team were already making their way down.

Hudson radioed for video on Shannon.

When she moved into position, he caught her arm, adding, "You know I have reservations. Please take my words seriously. I don't want you to push yourself. Not before you're ready. You'll pay for it in the end."

"But Dr. Rollins gave me the all clear weeks ago."

"Training to race requires much more than what can be seen on an MRI, on an X-ray or in physical therapy. You understand that. We've been over it. I'd like to see you smile again, and I want to keep it there."

He wanted to keep her skiing. That was all he'd meant.

And depending on what he saw today, he might just need to finish that conversation tonight. Maybe even kill her dreams. But did that desire flow from his need to coach her or a misplaced fear for her safety, which another coach who wasn't emotionally attached to her might not possess?

Ultimately, his control over the situation, over her life and career, went only so far. She could find another coach She didn't need him.

And maybe he was a little too afraid of that reality.

Shannon positioned herself for the slope. A smile cracked over the thoughtful, focused expression when suddenly she angled her head in Hudson's direction.

Looking for reassurance?

He nodded.

She turned her face to the slope again and shoved off. He watched her lithe form carving through the snow, sliding down the run and picking up speed. She didn't have it in her to ski anything but fast.

Hudson followed her, watching her performance, her every move as best he could while he focused on staying upright himself. He hung back, pushing into a stop so he could watch her knee and how it affected the rest of her moves when she neared the base of the run. He wished he could have been there yesterday to see her on Terminator, but he couldn't have watched her and skied the mountain, too.

A subtle shift to the right drew his attention. He could barely detect it, but she definitely favored her right leg.

Adapting.

In his mind, he saw her tumble down the slope again. He saw his sister taking the spill that left her paralyzed.

His back tensed....

And at the bottom of the slope, Shannon lost her balance and toppled.

Hudson's heart zip-lined.

Chapter 6

Late that evening, Hudson sat on the edge of the sofa near the fireplace in the great room of the Ridgewood Ski Lodge. The lights were low, and he'd stoked the fire, which now wrapped him in a warm glow. If only it could penetrate the cold recesses of his heart.

The ski crowds were gone, with only a lone couple back in a dark corner left to keep him company. Even the Rusty Nail and the coffee bar had closed for the night.

Hudson had a decision to make. He'd ignored things for too long, but he couldn't have known it would come to this.

Releasing a burdened sigh, he sank deep into the sofa, allowing the fire to mesmerize him. As the flames danced before his eyes, the memories from that day eight years ago played across his vision. His sister tumbling down the slope.

Everything that happened that day…her condition now…was his fault. Skiing was a relatively safe sport compared to other activities, but the high speeds of the downhill made it the most dangerous of the alpine-skiing events. He'd never forgiven himself for being the one to urge his sister on when she wasn't ready for it.

And then there was Shannon.

Thinking of her fall today, he squeezed his eyes shut. In the end, she'd picked herself up unaffected. But watching her tumble had a completely different effect on Hudson than on her. He was the one struggling to pick up the pieces. He was the one feeling the pain.

He couldn't do this anymore.

He had to let go of this situation. Of the memories and the blame.

Someone sat on the sofa, but he kept his eyes closed. He didn't want to engage. Couldn't they tell he needed time alone?

Just go home, Hudson.

He snuck a peek.

Shannon. His heart hammered. *Not now. Not...now...*

He should have gone home.

Steadying his breath, he opened his eyes and looked over. She studied him, her expression drawn.

"You didn't say anything," she said softly. "I thought you'd want to talk to me. Say something about warning me. Or feed me encouragement. Either way, something would have been better than nothing."

Did he hear pain in her voice? The emotional kind that trumped physical any day? His silence had hurt her.

He simply sat and stared, the words jumbled in his heart and head. Then, finally, "I'm not ready to talk."

Shannon shoved her red tresses away from her face. "You're my coach. Talking is what you do. I need to know what you're thinking."

"Does it matter?" What had gotten into him? He sounded like anything but her coach. Anything but a man who cared about her more than he had a right to care, in a way he shouldn't.

"Yes. It matters. You've been my coach for a long time. I trust you."

Hudson stared into the flames again. "If you trusted me, then why did you ski Terminator when I told you not to? No, don't answer that. It doesn't matter. What's done is done."

"What do you mean?"

"You're pushing too hard too fast. You might need to take a year, Shannon. Maybe two. If you have enough patience to go as slow as you need to go, and enough persistence to stick with it long enough, then you might get back on track. But right now, you're not there yet. You can't train yet, at least at the necessary racing speeds, without risking a worse injury."

An image of Jen's face, tears streaking down her cheeks as she lay perfectly still in the snow after her fall, suffused his mind. His pulse jumped up a notch. Pushing his emotions down to a manageable place, he risked a look at Shannon. Firelight leaped in the reflection of moisture filling her determined eyes.

"That's crazy. Jimmy Adams, Clint Riley, just to name a few. All experienced serious injuries after falling in the downhill. They're up and skiing again."

"Yeah, and there's Renee Holcomb and Jason Zimmerman, who weren't so fortunate." One dead from a head injury, the other paralyzed.

And there was Jennifer Landers. But he wouldn't bring her into this conversation. It had turned exceedingly more morbid than he'd intended.

"I don't get it. If you're so afraid then why are you even coaching?"

Hudson rubbed his temples. When he dropped his hand, Shannon's gaze probed his. Would she see in his eyes the truth? That he had feelings for her that went beyond what a coach should feel? That he couldn't watch her get hurt after what he'd been through? He wished he could tell her everything. But in the end, it wouldn't matter.

Someone else needed to coach her. He was no good for her anymore. No good for the rest of the team—he'd spent far too much energy worrying about her instead of being the coach the team needed.

A sigh escaped him. "You're right. You're absolutely right."

From the corner of his vision, he watched her rub her arms. The fire exuded warmth, but maybe he felt it more than she did. When she didn't respond, Hudson figured she waited for him to continue. To give her an explanation he was sure she wouldn't understand.

"I don't agree with the direction you're apparently determined to go." *I can't stand by and watch you get hurt.* He shouldn't tell her now. Not like this. Not before he'd done this officially, but then again, he understood how it would affect her to hear it from someone else. "I'm done."

"Hudson…what are you saying? You can't mean—"

"I'm resigning."

His words stunned her, sending shards of agony through her heart. "Because…of me?"

Spoken in haste, she regretted the words. His decision couldn't be because of her. There had to be more to it. Her pulse roared in her ears.

"No." Hudson stood and scraped both hands through his hair. "You don't understand."

And he obviously didn't understand that he'd just hurt her worse than anyone. The man had assured her he'd stay by her side, and now he was leaving. He wouldn't be the first. "I think I do."

"How could you?" he asked.

This wasn't the Hudson she knew. "When I fell and injured my leg and knee, my father was worried, of course. He loves me. But there was something else. He was disappointed and still is. He placed so much importance on my winning. My ski-racing career. And Jack dumped me...he *dumped* me, when I fell from the fast track. Look, maybe I'm being presumptuous here, maybe you're not resigning because of me, but I can't help but feel like you're disappointed in me, too."

"I'm not disappointed. Far from it," he said, his words distant.

Hudson moved to the fireplace and propped his arm on the mantel. His face was granite, preventing her from reading him. But if she knew anything about this man, she knew the deeply chiseled lines of his frown didn't mean he was cold or callous—he was in pain.

But why? And if not because of her, then what had happened to cause this reaction?

Shannon approached him and fought the urge to place her hand on his arm, his shoulder, his back, anywhere at all to connect with him. They were friends, if nothing else, weren't they? She wanted to keep her relationship with him. "Please, stay. Don't go."

Suddenly, he turned to her and cupped her face in his hands. Her breath caught in her throat as a powerful emotion she couldn't define swept over her.

He searched her eyes, a torrent of conflict waging war in his own. "I've made my decision. Now you have to make yours."

The way he looked at her now... Something stirred inside Shannon. Hudson—the man who'd stayed with her through the slow and painful rehabilitation after the fall. And the man who was willing to hang with her now if she would just take things slowly. She couldn't stand to push him away, to lose him like this. And yet, she couldn't abide the schedule he set before her. Shouldn't the decision be hers, in the end?

Behind his eyes, she could see he begged her to understand. Even to let him go. Shannon couldn't bear to look into his eyes any longer and closed hers. She fought to keep the quiver from her lips.

How could it have come to this, though? It seemed so drastic.

Slowly, he let his hands drop, but she could still feel their impression, the imprint of something she couldn't identify on her heart. She tried to stop her spinning thoughts. Calm her pounding heart.

She opened her eyes. This couldn't be about her. "But what about the team? Who will coach them?"

"We have assistant coaches for a reason. Jason is ready to be head coach, and if not, there's another coach your father has been hoping to attract to the team. I'm sure he's mentioned the man to you."

No. He hadn't. Shannon shrugged, not wanting to reveal that her father would keep anything from her, but it stung.

"He'll be better for you, Shannon. If racing and winning is in your blood and it's all you want in the world, then you need someone better than me."

Shannon couldn't find any words to respond. She took two steps back to put more space between them.

"Someone with decades of experience," he added. "I've taken you as far as I can."

You're wrong. Hudson was perfect for her. She didn't want anyone else to coach her despite her earlier traitorous thoughts. Thinking about them was one thing, reality another. Shannon fought the sensation that she was about to crumple inside and out.

If only they could find a compromise.

She shut her eyes. His musky cologne mingled with the scent of the fireplace and wrapped around her, giving her a sense of safety and comfort she hadn't known she'd needed.

When she opened her eyes, she noticed the way he stared at her, and Shannon's throat grew tight.

"What will you do now?" Her question broke through the quiet tension.

What if I need you?

How selfish she'd become. Obviously, the man needed this break. Maybe even had something better waiting for him. A step up from the Ridgewood Ski Team. Maybe he wasn't thinking about her at all.

He shrugged, releasing a half laugh, as if he was struggling to believe he was really doing this, just as Shannon was. As if he didn't really know what his next step was.

He moved away from her. "Don't worry. You haven't seen the last of me."

Then he did something completely out of character. He winked.

Coach Hudson Landers turned his back on her and walked out of the lodge.

Shannon slipped inside her bedroom and leaned against the wall, slumping to the floor. This misery was nothing like those initial moments days and weeks after her injury.

Was Hudson that important to her as a coach? Somehow she knew it was much more than that. The pain in her heart was palpable, and she pressed her hand against her chest.

Her coach was yet another person she'd disappointed. Only this time it was not because she was injured, but because she had the drive and motivation to overcome that injury. It made no sense.

Standing near the fireplace tonight, Shannon had the feeling this was all personal to him in some way. That *she* was personal to him. Gone was the invisible line that always seemed to stand between them and hold some part of him back from her.

And now more than that line was gone. *He* was gone. Shannon wasn't sure she could face the emptiness he left behind.

Chapter 7

As Hudson stood at the top of a ski run belonging to Ender's Peak Ski Resort, the distinct feeling that he had betrayed Ridgewood plowed over him, though he'd been gone two weeks now, and it was already the end of February. Considering his argument with Robert de Croix when he had resigned, he shouldn't have worried too much. Shannon's father didn't agree with Hudson about her training schedule, deciding to take her position, which served to confirm that Hudson's resignation had been the right decision. Robert had planned to bring in the new coach and keep Hudson on so he could focus his energy on Shannon.

The conversation lingered in Hudson's thoughts, making him tense all over. He rolled his shoulders to work the stiffness out. If the friction between them ever subsided, and he prayed it would, at some point in the future, maybe he could discuss the initiation of a ski program for the disabled at Ridgewood.

But right now, Shannon's father focused on his new

coach and what the man could do for their ski-program aspirations, the ski team and...for his daughter.

Hudson had left at exactly the right time. If he'd stayed on, his feelings for Shannon and the way they clouded his judgment might have become too obvious to the new coach. Hudson's leaving was best for everyone concerned. He would be forgotten soon enough. Though the decision had been one of the hardest of his life, it felt right. That was, if it weren't for that nagging feeling of betrayal.

Regardless of the reasons he left, the level at which Shannon wanted to ski required a team of world-class coaches and sports scientists—something she hadn't gotten at Ridgewood. In that way, her own father held her back. She could have already moved to Park City or some other training ground if she hadn't fallen, but things hadn't worked out that way, so Hudson was the one to leave.

He blew out a cloudy breath. Had to stop thinking about her.

Large, heavy flakes fell silently around him, sticking to his face as he watched a volunteer helping Reggie, a three-track disabled skier who'd lost his left leg. His one ski was full size and his special poles, or outriggers, had small skis on the ends, giving the man three points of contact on the snow.

From Hudson's previous months working as a volunteer with the program, he already knew most of the people involved. Both the volunteers and the disabled. That made for an easier transition, but he couldn't simply forget the friends he'd made at Ridgewood.

He hadn't been back since the day he'd said goodbye to the other coaches, friends and the ski-racing team he'd trained for four years. There hadn't been a lot of time to say much, because the team was headed out to a regional competition.

They'd miss him, he believed, but they were also excited about what the future would hold with such a decorated coach to lead them—he knew, because he'd made sure they understood what they were getting. The last thing he'd ever wanted was to leave with anyone holding bad feelings toward him, so he'd done as much damage control as he could, but maybe not enough.

Unfortunately, Shannon had become a casualty in more than one way. During his mini farewell party, she'd stood back, kept her distance. Just as well. But her reaction that day hadn't kept her from his thoughts. He recalled the moment by the fireplace when he told her he was resigning. Remembering the flames reflecting in her soft gaze, he shut his eyes to envision her auburn hair falling in tangles across her shoulders.

For a moment, he thought she might have seen in his eyes what he felt for her. He'd struggled then, wanting her to understand, and yet he couldn't let her know. Even so, he'd shown her some of his affection when he'd cupped the soft skin of her face in his palms.

Obviously she didn't think of him like that. It was for the best. He didn't deserve anyone's love, and now that he wouldn't see Shannon every day, he could stick to his resolve.

He'd told her that she hadn't seen the last of him, because he couldn't bear to think of ending their relationship completely. Couldn't bear to see the hurt in her eyes. Even though his gut churned thinking about someone else coaching her, he'd stay away, keep his distance.

If only he could do that in his mind. The doubts bombarded him. Would the new coach understand Shannon the way Hudson did? Would he care enough about her to protect her? To deny her, for her own safety, if necessary, as Hudson had done? He reminded himself that the answers to these questions were no longer his concern, a path he'd chosen with good reason.

He was on a new course. Would his sister, Jen, agree with his decision? His deep-seated need to make everything right, though that was an attempt at the impossible? Maybe somehow if he spent enough time and worked hard enough he could redeem his past.

God knew he hadn't forgiven himself.

He needed to make the trip to see Jen, like he did every few months. He would never have left her side if she hadn't begged him to go. To live his life and let her live her own.

Forcing his thoughts back to his new job as director of the disabled program, Hudson hiked over to assist some volunteers helping someone on a dual ski. In the distance, a familiar feminine form made trails in the thick falling snow toward him. Amanda had asked him to meet her at the lodge, but she'd been delayed, and he'd busied himself with the volunteers and forgotten about their meeting until that moment.

"You have that contemplative look on your face," she said, stomping her boots next to him. "You don't already regret your decision to join us, do you?"

"Of course not." Hudson watched as the volunteer coaches assisted the student with the dual ski into the chairlift. "I won't lie to you. It's hard starting over."

"Oh, but you're not starting over. You're starting at the top. You don't know it, but I was grooming you to become director this whole time." She chuckled. "You're great with people. With the kids. No doubt there. But I was hoping to have this conversation inside while I held a warm cup of joe."

Grinning, she rubbed her gloveless hands together.

"Sure. Let's go." Hudson returned her smile and wished he meant it all the way through. It hadn't been easy, leaving a place—and people—he loved for a new opportunity, even though it was one he wanted.

The snowfall thickened around them as he tromped beside Amanda down the short incline to the lodge. This was his future.

A future without Shannon de Croix in his life. He cared about her enough to do what was best for her.

Shannon forced her eyes to the new head coach, Stefan Hofler—from Austria, no less—and away from the snow-packed hills that dazzled her from the other side of the floor-to-ceiling windows. She and the rest of the Ridgewood Ski Team were packed in the conference room, made to sit there for hours when they should be out on the slopes. Made to listen to Coach Hofler pontificate about his new techniques and strategies. Ranting about how things would be different around here.

Jason and the other four assistant coaches stood against the wall, but she couldn't read any of them. Did they agree with this new stuff? Or did they have a choice? She thought Jason had been positioned to become head coach. Was he upset that he was upstaged by Coach Hofler? The Ridgewood board along with her father had taken great pains to bring in a world-class coach with decades of experience. All part of Daddy's dream for his resort and ski team.

She wanted to know why the new head coach thought Ridgewood needed a different strategy. Had Hudson known that Coach Hofler's techniques would conflict with his own? Maybe that was the real reason he left. He couldn't counter both her father and this man.

Hudson placed importance on smiling and having fun.

Coach Hofler was about winning at any cost. About throwing out safety and patience in order to win, stating cautious skiing didn't produce excellence or fame. Racers should push to win or fall down the mountain trying.

Her mantra exactly.

Shannon should be happy.

Instead, salty moisture surged at the corners of her eyes. She was anything but happy.

Next to her, Rodney yawned quietly. Once again, her gaze drifted to the slopes filled with recreational skiers. Maybe she could watch them and still focus on the man's words. He'd positioned her to train with the team again with none of Hudson's reservations. Made her feel as if she was one of them. And she'd wanted that, hadn't she?

During practice yesterday, they had all been a little confused, not understanding what the man expected, hence today's lecture. An ache had coursed through her knee, throwing her a little off. Hudson would have questioned her, and though he might have said nothing at all about her knee, she would have known he understood what was going on. She would have *felt* his concern for her.

Hudson Landers, for all the frustration she'd endured over the past few weeks before he left, had given her his attention. Maybe even his full attention—she saw that now.

Hofler focused on skiing together and winning as a team. He didn't bother to single out those who might have potential to move on. Was that what her father and the board wanted?

Shannon dragged her hands through her hair, feeling more off course than ever.

"Miss de Croix. Did you hear me?" Coach Hofler's words, spoken with an accent, jolted her upright.

"Of course."

He stared at her momentarily, the attention he now decided to bestow on her leaving her humiliated. Thank goodness he didn't say more to her. Instead he discussed the upcoming races left in the season, races for which Shannon wouldn't be ready despite training hard again. The fall had changed her life, thrown her off track in ways she couldn't have imagined. She was bruised on the inside as well as the outside, and she hadn't realized what

Hudson had brought to the team, and to her, until it was too late. But somehow, she'd have to grow accustomed to Coach Stefan Hofler from Austria.

Finally, he dismissed them so they could train, implementing the drive and ambition he expected to see exhibited on the slopes. As members of the team exited through the conference-room door, she couldn't help but notice not one single person seemed happy at the new training strategies.

Shannon stood at the bottleneck as everyone filed out, sensing Coach Hofler's eyes on her. When it was her turn to move through the door, he thrust his hand out enough to block her.

"A word, please?" he asked.

When everyone had left the room, including the other coaches, Coach Hofler closed the door, imprisoning Shannon in the mini conference room with him.

She eyed the coach, the wrong attitude blooming in her chest. She didn't like him.

At all.

"You're a star student on this team and they look up to you. That is the foremost reason why I want you training right alongside the rest of them. I don't do things the way Coach Landers did."

No kidding.

"I don't need a diva on the ski team. Understood?"

Shannon caught her gasp. Where had that come from? Just who did he think he was talking to? Did he realize her father founded the ski-team organization and this resort? A string of ugly words exploded in her mind, but she contained them. "I understand."

He nodded. Shannon shoved through the door to freedom. She'd have a word with her father about this. With the thought, realization dawned.

I really do act like a diva.

That was not what she'd wanted or intended. Not at all.

Tears threatened behind her eyes. Shannon held them in check and worked through the afternoon with her fellow team skiers, adhering to the new coach's protocols. She could do this.

If there was one thing she read in his eyes, it was that he would hold back her career if he didn't like her. He'd do it for far different reasons than either her father or Hudson.

At the end of training, Shannon didn't hang around long enough for the new coach to speak to her again. Instead, she fled to the cabin, shedding her skiwear as she made her way through the living room, down the hallway then finally to her bedroom. She slammed the door and let all the tears and anger loose.

Swiping at her wet cheeks, she loathed herself at the moment. Hated her life. But that was wrong, and this wasn't how things were supposed to be. She had a very blessed life. Curling into a ball, she released all the rest and let God hear her cries, whispering her secret anguish to Him. After all, He knew everything already, anyway. No matter what she did, she couldn't seem to do things right. Make people happy. She was messing everything up. She felt as if even God wasn't happy with her. But she wasn't happy with Him, either. He'd let her fall, hadn't He? The despondent thoughts warred in her soul, the angst pouring from her heart as the tears streamed from her eyes. This wasn't what she wanted or where she wanted to be.

How do I get back on track, God?

A soft knock on the door woke her—at some point in her despair she'd fallen asleep. Darkness stared back at her from the window.

The knock came again, accompanied by her father's gentle voice. "Shannon?"

She sat up and swiped away any remnant of dried, salty tears.

"Come in," she said. It seemed she was a little girl again.

The door eased open and in stepped her father, his expression somber. She obviously hadn't done a good job of hiding her distress.

"What's wrong?" he asked.

"Nothing." *Everything.* Her father had created this...this kingdom for her to ski and she was ruining everything.

He entered her room and switched on a lamp, then sat in the plush pink chair in the corner. She *was* a little girl, still living with her father at twenty-two. But their living arrangements made sense for their lives.

"Don't lie to me," he said, his words soft. "Tell me what's going on."

"What am I doing here, Daddy?"

He opened his mouth to speak but hesitated, then finally said, "What do you mean?"

"I feel like my life is off track. I'm getting a little old, don't you think, to keep chasing after these ski-racing dreams?" *Your ski-racing dreams.*

"Are you feeling all right?" His eyes twinkled, matching his teasing grin.

"I'm serious."

"It's the new coach, isn't it?"

Shannon nodded, again feeling like a diva. "He's not for me. We don't get along. It's not like it was with Hudson." Even though she felt as if he'd held her back, she understood he'd wanted her to be patient in her recovery. She'd been anything but, and she'd run him off. Or had it been about her at all? Now that she thought about it, everything appeared as if she thought the world revolved around her and her alone. But that wasn't it, was it?

Her father scratched the stubble on his chin. "I thought I could grow this place, bring in the right people to make it the kind of facility you needed. So you could stay close. Train here and stay with me."

He pushed to his feet and jammed his hands into his pockets, paced her room. "But you need to train hard. You need a coach to focus on you and travel to the races with you. Landers tried to give you as much attention as he could, but he had a whole team to think about. Maybe you need a private coach."

"But, Daddy, that would cost more money."

"True," he said and leaned over to kiss her forehead. "But you're worth it. Besides, that's what sponsors are for."

"Just bring Hudson back. Convince him to work with the team or with me, however you have to get him back." Shannon leaned forward, pressing her face into her hands. "Oh, great. Now I really do sound like a diva."

Her father chuckled. "You're no diva. Don't even say that. And Landers, I won't bring him back. He has issues."

At the comment, she looked up. "What do you mean?"

"Things in his life, in his past, that drive him."

"You've got my attention now. Tell me."

"I didn't bring that up so I could divulge things I'm sure he'd prefer kept private, but to warn you, he's not the best coach for you. His techniques worked for us for a while, but he and I both knew it was time for him to move on."

"I don't understand. A few weeks ago you told me to listen to him." Shannon stood to face her father. "Where did he go?"

Her father stared down at her. Then he turned and walked out of the room, shaking his head as he went. "He's not coming back here."

Why? Because her father wouldn't let him? Or because Hudson wouldn't come back even if she agreed to abide by his terms? She recalled the day he'd said goodbye. Shannon had stood back in the corner, feeling guilty and ashamed. She'd disconnected her emotions, distanced herself from the whole situation as he gave his impromptu farewell speech. Listening to him, she thought she might burst out in tears, and she couldn't do that in front of everyone.

What had he said? Something about working with disabled kids. To come see him. She knew he volunteered several times a year. Why hadn't she just gotten over it and paid more attention?

That was a start.

Hudson.

She fell back on the bed and thought about the night he'd told her he was leaving. How he'd looked at her.

And that was when she realized—he was more to her than simply her coach. Exactly what, she wasn't sure yet.

A warm feeling started in her heart and grew. For the first time in weeks, she felt a hope she hadn't even known she'd lost. Hudson didn't have to come here. She would go to him…once she found out where he'd gone. For all she knew, he'd be at a bigger, better ski-training facility, but working in an adaptive ski program. But it didn't matter where he'd gone. She would find him.

He understood her like no one else. Always read her so well—she missed the connection she had with him. Funny that they understood each other the way they did, and yet Hudson kept the wall up just enough. A wall he'd put in place to define the lines between students and coach. Could that be why she'd failed to recognize that he meant more to her?

I have to find him. The only problem was, what if he didn't want to be found?

Chapter 8

Shannon pulled into a parking space at Ender's Peak Ski Resort, Cecile by her side.

Squeezing the steering wheel of her silver Camry, Shannon stared at one of the biggest lodges and ski resorts she'd ever seen—one of the most popular in New Mexico. Her father's competition—and Hudson had come here? No wonder her father didn't want him back.

"You sure about this?" Cecile asked.

"I'm sure I don't want my father to know we came here." She hated keeping secrets from him. They'd always been close. But apparently he'd kept a few from her, too. Still, the reasons she'd come here today had nothing to do with this ski resort, his competition.

"Let's do this." She opened the door and climbed out.

Cecile caught up with her around the front of the vehicle and together they headed to the ski area. "How do you know he's even working today?"

Shannon sent a hard stare Cecile's way. "You're the one

who told me what he was up to. You, who always asks the right questions as you serve hot chocolate to your customers."

Shannon believed she knew Hudson, understood him, but she didn't know that much about him. He kept his private life…well, private.

"True, but I don't know his hours."

"Let's assume they are eight to five and hope for the best." With her first step forward, her pulse skipped erratically. She'd left her gloves behind, and despite the frigid temperature, her hands perspired in her pockets.

"You don't think he'll see you as a stalker type, do you?" Cecile asked.

Shannon knew Cecile well enough to know she'd meant to tease with her comment. Even so, she wasn't sure how Hudson would see the situation.

"Let's hope not. But first, I'll watch him from a distance. He won't see me yet."

"Right." Cecile chuckled. "You're no stalker."

Nausea swirled in Shannon's stomach as she trudged through the snow around the resort, which was crowded with recreational skiers in their brightly colored pants and jackets, though black seemed to be the color of the day. "I just want to see him. Talk to him. Say I'm sorry and wish him well. I didn't really get to do that." She should have done that when she'd had the chance. But she didn't know then what she knew now.

Sporting an official Ender's Peak jacket, a young woman with frizzy brown hair walked in their direction. Shannon's pulse jumped to her throat. She envisioned the woman barring her from entering the ski resort because she was a spy from the competition. Shannon shoved the crazy, panic-born thoughts aside and steadied her breaths. The rapid puffs of white clouds gave away too much.

When the woman passed, Shannon caught her arm. "Excuse me, I'm looking for Coach Landers?"

The ski-resort employee smiled, twisted and pointed behind her. "Just up there. He's assisting his students on the Grove Hill ski run."

"Thanks." Shannon released her and started toward the lifts and ski runs, but with so many, chances were good she'd need a map.

"Uh, but he doesn't like to be disturbed during the classes. He's the director, and he trains the coaches and students. You should wait until it's over."

Shannon hadn't realized he was the director. "When's it done?"

The woman looked at her watch. "Another fifteen minutes."

Shannon nodded. "Thanks again," she said.

"Anytime." The woman continued on her way.

"Wow, the director." She was impressed. The chances that he would come back to Ridgewood dropped significantly, though they were never very good. What was she doing here?

She kept going but Cecile didn't follow.

She turned to look at her friend. "You coming?"

"I'm going to check things out inside. See how they run their restaurant and coffee bar. Besides, I think this is something you need to do without me tagging along like a third wheel, or more like your nosy mother."

"More like an older sister." Shannon sighed. "You don't think I should do this, do you?"

"I didn't say that. In fact, I think you're doing the right thing."

Shannon smiled. "Thanks, I needed to hear that. I value your opinion."

"And I needed to hear *that*. Now go find your dream

coach." Cecile left Shannon and headed toward the grand entrance of the Ender's Peak Ski Resort.

After she'd hiked a hundred yards, Shannon paused to take in the vastness of the mountain base, the lifts and what she could see of the ski runs, too many to count. But she couldn't see Hudson working with the disabled students from here. She'd have to get much closer to where he was. Her palms grew moist again. What had she been thinking to come here today? She had no idea what she would say to him, and if anything, the feeling she'd made a mistake nagged at her, especially when she thought back to her father's words about Hudson. He'd said Hudson had issues. What were they?

Since she'd come all this way and was here now, she wouldn't let the doubts keep her from Hudson. Pulling her jacket tighter, she hiked through the snow, wondering if she'd have more success finding him if she put on skis. Then she spotted him, wearing the same attire she'd seen him in a hundred times, only this time he wasn't wearing skis.

Shannon's heart skipped, and she couldn't decide if that was because she was unsure of how he'd react to seeing her, or something more.

The day was hazy and thick with snowfall, and he'd donned goggles instead of sunglasses. But they were perched on his black knit cap, instead of the helmet he usually wore when he actively skied.

Shannon hiked up the hill to get closer and found a grove of trees nearby where she could hang back out of sight and watch.

Yeah. Cecile was right. She was a stalker. Inside, she cringed at the thought, feeling like an idiot on the one hand and glad she was here on the other.

Hudson stood with two volunteer coaches, one of whom held a tether attached to a student on skis sitting in a chair.

Shannon leaned against an evergreen heavy with snow and slipped her hands into her pockets to keep them warm. She thought of the day she'd hid in the trees waiting for Hudson and the team to ride the ski lift up the mountain. She wasn't hiding from him this time, but she wasn't exactly sure she wanted him to discover that she was watching him.

His voice, strong yet gentle at the same time, drifted over to her as he spoke to the two coaches and the boy in the chair, who looked about ten. Shannon had always believed Hudson was a great coach, but she saw now that he really had a special way with kids.

She listened as he told a joke and chuckled. The boy's laughter joined with Hudson's and resounded through the trees where Shannon stood watching. Then Hudson's tone grew serious, and she could just make out the words, encouraging words—that despite his disability, the boy could accomplish anything he wanted. All he had to do was adapt.

The words sent her back to that day when she'd joined the team unannounced. Hudson had used that same word with her.

Adapt.

He continued his dialog with the student, encouraging him to be patient. Not to push himself. The weight of an avalanche pressed against her chest—she was back, listening to him telling her the same things. Encouraging her. But she hadn't wanted to hear. And now she watched him coaching someone else, *somewhere* else.

Of all the outcomes of her pressing desire to accelerate her training schedule, she never could have imagined she'd push her coach away. Still, he seemed as comfortable here as he had been at Ridgewood.

He had a way with kids.

A way with disabled kids.

Elizabeth Goddard

And he *had* a way with her. She hadn't known what she had until she'd lost it. Until she'd driven him away.

It was hard to imagine life without him around and especially difficult to imagine her regaining her racing career without his guidance.

Coach Hofler didn't make her feel special. He wasn't patient and caring. Nor did he believe in her the way Hudson had. Though she admitted her thoughts were selfish, how would she race again? She couldn't see herself as a serious competitor without Hudson Landers by her side.

She blinked back the unshed tears when a blurred figure drew near, pulling her from her angst.

Hudson.

He hiked toward her. What happened to his class? His student? The volunteers were already skiing toward the resort. Shannon had been too lost in her thoughts to notice the class was over. To notice when Hudson had caught her watching him.

Despite the cold temperature, heat suffused her neck and face. Why it should matter, she wasn't sure, but for an instant she wanted to shrink behind the trees and become invisible. Even so, she'd sought him out, hadn't she? Shannon shoved from the tree and stood tall, hoping her smile would set the tone. He crunched through the snow to stand beside her. She hadn't stood this close to him in weeks, and she was suddenly overwhelmed by how much she had missed him.

His slate-blue eyes, so serious and wary, assessed her.

That was disappointing—she'd hoped he would be glad to see her.

"Shannon," he said. His voice wrapped around her, squeezing her heart. "What are you doing here?"

When he'd first noticed her watching him from the trees, his chest had constricted. He had struggled to breathe, but he'd shoved it aside to focus on Jeremy, his student. Great kid. Determined. Focused—just like Hudson needed to be. Today served as a clear reminder of just why he needed to distance himself from Shannon and the Ridgewood Ski Lodge—he hadn't been the coach the team needed.

Now that he stood here facing her, his attention freed up, his lungs definitely labored for oxygen again. Why her? Why this girl?

Her plans, her dreams, would take her in the opposite direction—a world away from him. He needed to disassociate himself from that future.

She cleared her throat and glanced away, but said nothing in reply to his question. She'd sought him out, which meant she wanted something from him. Finally, she pulled her gloveless hands from her pockets and rubbed them together as if that would help her work up the nerve to speak.

"I came to see you. What else?"

Huh? That hadn't even occurred to him. Unfortunately, he didn't believe it. Couldn't be that simple.

Hudson shifted his weight and glanced at his watch. He eyed the resort a short distance away at the bottom of the incline. "I have a class in an hour and a half. Let's get you inside with a warm drink. Then you can tell me why you're here."

He hated that he sounded so harsh.

Shannon sighed. "Look, I'm sorry if I disrupted your day—"

"I'm glad you came," he interrupted. He was. Sort of. "I didn't mean to sound like I wasn't. But I figure you must have a reason, that's all." Before he said anything else that sounded stupid, he started toward the resort and lodge that housed a couple of eateries.

Shannon crunched in the snow next to him. Happy chatter, screams of delight and the sound of skis slicing through the powder echoed around him. These were the sounds he knew, the sounds that he was most familiar with. Where he felt at home. It shouldn't matter where he coached or whom he coached.

And the girl next to him, the way he was aware of her presence, of her every move, threw him off balance. His whole day was likely shot, but a smile edged into his lips anyway.

Shannon came to a stop. "Oh, the aerial tramway." A small gasp escaped her. "I…"

Hudson paused with her to stare at the entrance to the tram across the way.

A sheepish grin flashed across her face. She glanced at him, then shrugged and kept walking.

"Wait." He grabbed her, holding her back. "What about it?"

"My father always hoped to add one or at least a gondola at Ridgewood, but he never got to that. Not yet."

Hudson figured Shannon had ridden in her share of them when she traveled to various locales for the races she had competed in, but he couldn't be sure. Even so, she hadn't ridden *this* one with the most amazing panoramic vistas—*that* he was sure of by her reaction. Nor would her father want her fraternizing with the enemy. Though, to be fair, her father was on friendly terms with the resort owners.

But then it hit him.

"He doesn't know you're here, does he?" Not that it mattered. She was an adult. Right. It mattered anyway. And this could be the only chance she had to enjoy the ride.

She shrugged.

"Come on." Suddenly infused with a crazy urge to show her something new, he tugged on her arm, hoping she'd follow him to the entrance. Couldn't risk dragging her by the hand. Needed to keep what little control over the situation he had left in check.

"Wait! Where are you going?"

"The tramway. Where else?" he called over his shoulder, confident she would follow.

"What about that warm drink?"

He slowed and turned to face her. "Your choice. Warm drink? Or tramway?" he asked, though he planned to deliver hot chocolate at the restaurant on top. Would she guess?

"That's hardly fair," she said and took the lead with a smile, jamming her hands into her pockets.

What he was doing, he didn't know. Didn't care. He just knew he wanted to see the delight in Shannon de Croix's eyes again. See the kind of smiles he'd seen on her face before she'd taken that fall.

While under his care and direction.

Once at the aerial tramway station, they waited in a shorter line than could be found on the weekends and then crowded into the tram until it was standing-room only, people packed like too many skis in a locker. Loud chatter filled the space. A bell resounded, reminding Hudson of the San Francisco cable cars.

Pressed together by the throng of sightseers, Hudson stood closer to Shannon than he'd ever been. This hadn't been a good idea, after all, but he shoved the doubts aside and gently ushered her from the center of the tram closer to a window. She was already familiar with spectacular views, he knew that, but not like this—not from this vantage point, looking down on the rocky, snow-crusted hills of the Sangre de Cristo Mountains.

The tram slowly rose over a deep canyon, rocks emerging from the snow in places. He almost wished they'd done this at sunrise or sunset. He leaned in to whisper, "You know they say the mountains were named for the blood of Christ."

She nodded. "I'm familiar with alpenglow, when the sun

reflects off the mountains and creates a red band, hits the snow at just the right angle and the peaks look red, too."

She slid a sideways glance his way. "I'm sure it's amazing from up here, though."

A lady next to Shannon gasped and pointed out the window, drawing Shannon's attention. At Shannon's small intake of breath, Hudson fought to breathe himself. But not because of the view.

When they reached the top and the end of the ride, Shannon—a girl born to the mountains and the majestic scenery—appeared a little dazed. As if she was in awe. The group filed out of the tram, and when Hudson stepped out before Shannon, he couldn't help himself: he took her hand to assist her down. Any gentleman would have done the same.

But he wasn't just any gentleman. She wasn't just any girl.

Placing her small, soft hand in his, she smiled and her cheeks brightened. Or had they? They were already red from the cold, but had the color deepened?

"And now for that warm drink," he said, feeling as if this had turned into something much more than a simple ride on the tramway, but that thinking had to be completely one-sided.

"Oh, you." She pulled her hand free and jabbed him in the arm. "You planned that all along."

"So what if I did?"

Being with her scrambled his brain cells so he couldn't think straight. Hence, he was on what felt more like a mini date with her. He started for the restaurant, and she walked beside him, wrapping her arms around herself. He couldn't exactly hug her to him to ward off the chill of the higher elevation.

What am I doing? He'd meant to distance himself from

her. But by showing up today, she was twisting everything around. Entangling him again.

"Thanks for this. It's…breathtaking."

I was thinking the same thing. Hudson watched her as she looked at the panoramic view of the mountain range, Santa Fe in the distance.

Once inside the restaurant, they settled into a booth and ordered hot drinks in big mugs. He glanced at his watch, wishing he had more time. He was pressing this as it was.

"Now, what did you want to see me about?" He injected as much warmth as he could into his smile, but the question still seemed a little off, considering the last few moments he'd shared with her.

He'd never forget them. In truth, he didn't care why she'd wanted to see him. She was here.

In the face of this fantasy scenery, he needed a reality check. They held warm mugs in their hands, and again Hudson could almost envision himself on a date with her. Almost. But that wasn't what was on her mind, and he needed to quit torturing himself with what he couldn't and shouldn't have.

She looked into her cup, steam floating into her face. "I wanted to see you. I…missed you."

This would be hard, but he needed to know. "As your coach? A friend? What?"

She grew serious then, and the magic was all gone. His fault.

"You're making this harder than it has to be," she said. "I missed you as a friend and, yes, as my coach, too. Is that a crime?"

Disappointment boiled inside him. He gazed into his own creamy chocolate brew. What answer was he expecting?

"Your students. Helping the disabled. What you're doing. It's amazing."

Her words tugged at something in his heart, and he looked up. Searched her gaze. For what, he wasn't sure. Before he'd left Ridgewood, he'd hoped to convince her to volunteer with him.

At least this was a topic he was comfortable with. "Makes me feel like I'm making a difference," he said. As if he'd finally found where he was supposed to be. There was so much more to it.

But he couldn't tell her he felt guilty. Ashamed. That after his sister's accident he viewed everything differently. He thought he was doing the right thing by coaching Shannon and the Ridgewood Ski Team, but he could hardly tell her that it was her blind drive to win at any cost that opened his eyes. It reminded him too much of himself.

Despite everything else that stood between them, that was the biggest of all.

"My father is considering bringing on another coach. Someone to help me train."

Dread churned in his gut. "A private coach, you mean. Hofler isn't working out?"

"For the team, sure. Just not for me."

Don't ask me to come back. Don't ask me. The look in her eyes—she wanted him to be the first to speak. She wanted him to offer to help her.

I can't. How did he make her understand? He didn't want to hurt her. "I'm sorry you don't think he's a good fit." He didn't dare ask her who her father had in mind, though he knew it wasn't him. It might open the door just enough, and she might be bold enough to ask. He didn't want this day to end with him turning her down flat.

The truth was, there was nothing he wanted more than to coach her. To make sure she didn't push too far and too fast. To keep her safe. He could hardly stand to think of someone else pushing her for his or her own gain. How could he trust anyone else with the task? But he reminded himself it wasn't his burden. He had enough guilt on his shoulders.

"I'm sorry to hear that." Hudson stared out the window at the tram. "I hate to cut this short, but I need to get back."

"Oh, sure." Her voice cracked a little. Subtle, but it was there. "I'm glad you could spend a few minutes talking. That's all I wanted. And the aerial tramway was an experience I'll never forget."

Me, either.

Somehow, he'd hurt her anyway. He could tell by the shift in her expression, her clouded eyes. Beautiful hazelgreen eyes that matched the trees. She was a vision.

How would he wipe today from his memory?

On the return ride, the tram was as crowded as it had been on the ride up. Hudson and Shannon watched the view. Any conversation was too hard without privacy, though talking would have been difficult, anyway. She seemed as burdened as he was.

He almost lost her as the throng exited the tram. When he spotted her, he called out.

She swung around to him. "Hey."

An awkward silence hung in the air. She glanced around as if she wasn't sure what to say or do.

He knew why she'd come, but he sensed somewhere deep down that maybe it was more than about him coaching her. Sheesh. How could he even think that? He was deluded.

"I'm glad you came to see me." And he was.

They were friends, like she said, weren't they? Whether he coached her or not. Shannon didn't have a clue about how he felt. That was only one of the reasons he'd left Ridgewood. He'd planned to keep it that way, over time extracting himself from her life completely. But he now saw how difficult that would be if Shannon didn't let go.

Again, the thought of another coach pushing her too

hard, risking her safety, raked over him. Maybe…maybe he could be a positive influence in her life in a different way. Help her find out who she was besides a downhill racer.

It was a risk. He had to count the cost. Was it worth it? Could he guard his heart?

He didn't know. And right now as he gazed into her shimmering, expectant eyes, he didn't care.

"I have Wednesday off. If it doesn't interfere with your training schedule, want to go snowshoeing with me?"

Chapter 9

Hudson shoved up his sunglasses and watched his breath puff out in white clouds. Sunlight reflected off the snow, causing him to squint.

Although most snowshoers preferred the Hyde Park Road trail, Hudson preferred something closer to home. Plus, he had the freedom to wander off the familiar trails and create his own. Doing that here didn't run the risk of triggering a snowslide.

He'd given Shannon the address where they were to meet, and she'd assured him she knew her way. But here he stood. Alone. Snowshoes strapped on. He waited a few feet from where he'd parked his Ford Explorer near the trail head. He'd left a voice mail on her cell phone and hoped she was okay. Why he thought she would show up, he didn't know. He was crazy to invite her to begin with. A moment of insanity.

Just as well.

Hudson shoved off to enjoy his second favorite sport,

this one all about taking things slow, experiencing nature—and life—rather than racing past it. If he hadn't invited Shannon, he could have expected his morning jaunt to leave him refreshed, exhilarated and relaxed. In tune with nature and God.

Instead, he moved with a heavy heart, forcing each of his snowshoed steps forward.

Forget about her. If he didn't, the day would be shot. He left his vehicle well behind and was a thousand feet down the trail when he heard another snowshoer coming up on him.

"Hey!" The familiar feminine voice called from behind. "Wait up!"

A grin he felt to his toes buried his troubled thoughts. Hudson hesitated for a moment, but kept moving. He didn't need her seeing his enthusiasm, did he? Besides, he'd make her work for it.

He focused on the white ground beneath his snowshoes and forced his smile away.

"Hey…Hudson!" she called again. "It's me. I made it."

She came after him, but couldn't catch up as he increased his speed. Though this wasn't meant to be a race, he supposed racing was in both his and Shannon's blood. He couldn't help himself. His competitive streak took over.

He'd kept up his pace for another hundred yards, not much in the world of ski racing or even jogging, but snowshoeing? How long could they keep at it before either of them would give in?

Her breaths came faster as she gained on him. Then Hudson remembered—he hadn't meant to challenge her like this. Racing on snowshoes was hard on the tendons and joints.

What if she further injured her knee?

Idiot. He should know better.

Hudson slowed to allow Shannon to catch up. She

crunched through the snow, still breathing a little hard for an athlete, and slapped him on the arm.

"What was that for?" he asked, knowing full well.

Shannon gifted him with her gorgeous, full-on smile. "You know. You didn't even start running until you heard me behind you."

"What's a little race between friends?" He winked. There. He'd said it. He hadn't intended to use the word, but that was what he wanted for them. If he was going to do this thing with her, instead of staying away, then he wanted to be something besides her coach.

He waited.

Her reaction meant everything.

She angled her head, her auburn hair spilling from the blue-and-green Nordic cap she wore. "Right. What's a little race between friends?"

He liked the playful tone lacing her words, the dimples edging into her cheeks, a little too much.

He tried to remember why he'd invited her today, besides the fact he wanted her along—but there was something, some reason beyond his pure selfishness at wanting to be with her. Her smile made him forget everything else.

"Ready?"

She nodded. "As I'll ever be."

Hudson faced the trail and hiked through the unadulterated part of the woods, where the snow was deep and undisturbed. Shannon kept pace with him, sometimes behind him, and other times she hiked next to him, but neither of them said anything. Together they enjoyed the serenity and muted silence of the snow-blanketed environment. His worries could easily fade away against the peaceful backdrop of the natural scenery.

Even though he wanted to forge a friendship that had nothing at all to do with the competitive-skiing world, he couldn't help the thoughts that bombarded him. And now he remembered the reason he'd invited her—to forge that friendship, not only for himself, but because he wanted to help her. To guide her from a distance, if possible. Maintaining a prudent balance between his new world and hers would be difficult. Sustaining a protective layer around his heart, even more so.

As she trekked beside him, he was aware of her decidedly feminine, athletic form. A million questions screamed in his head. He wanted to know about her training. About Hofler. Had her father found her a private coach yet? On the other hand, he didn't want to know.

Knowing could drive him nuts.

Asking could end this moment they shared.

One glance at Shannon and the look on her face told him she felt it, too. This had been a good idea, after all. As good for her as it was for him, even though he'd initially feared bringing her to the place where he enjoyed his alone time.

The trail narrowed, and Shannon moved behind him. A jackrabbit zipped in front of them, darting between trees and finally hiding in the foliage. Hudson knew when Shannon no longer followed. He stopped, too, and turned to check on her.

"You okay?" he asked.

She stared ahead at the place where the rabbit had dashed. "I've never done this before."

"What? Snowshoe? Or hike in the woods?"

"Either. I've never done either."

Hudson didn't know what to say. "I'm sorry to hear that." He hoped she was enjoying it, but maybe he'd read her wrong.

The rabbit moved from its hiding place and hopped away.

"Look." She smiled. "There it goes."

Turning his head, he followed where she pointed and watched the rabbit. "It's running away. We scared it," he said.

He glanced at her, hoping he wouldn't do the same thing to her.

She closed the short distance between them. Peering up at him, her eyes crystal clear in the brilliant day, she frowned. "Why didn't you wait for me?"

Chest tightening, he buried the emotions away before she could see in his eyes how much he cared.

"I didn't think you'd come," he said, mustering a non-chalant tone.

Hudson pushed on, putting them back on the official trail. They had to make another two miles around the loop before they circled and headed back.

Catching up, Shannon squeezed next to him on the narrow track. "That's my fault. I'm sorry I was late."

"No harm done. You said you'd never done this. What do you think?"

"I love it. I don't know why Daddy never took me. I guess we just spent so much time on skis, never had time to try other sports." She sighed. "Never took the time to just…explore."

Hudson didn't miss the regret in her words.

"How long have you been into snowshoeing?" she asked.

"As long as I can remember." An ache coursed through him with the memory of time spent with his sister.

He tensed. He'd said too much, even though he hadn't mentioned Jen. But he didn't want Shannon asking too many questions. He'd kept his personal life to himself for a reason, never talking about it with his students or anyone at Ridgewood Lodge. He wasn't free to share until he'd dealt with the guilt and pain. He wasn't ready to lay things out there for all to see until he had. Getting closer to Shannon would be risky on more than one front.

Even so, with her vibrant form next to him, the risks didn't fully register.

"I had to rent these snowshoes. I won't lie—it felt a little funny renting from the Ender's ski shop."

"You didn't get them at Ridgewood?"

"How could I? If I rented at Ridgewood then the guy who runs that shop might mention that to Daddy."

Hudson paused to catch his breath. Shannon stopped and faced him, waiting. He swiped the back of his gloved hand across his forehead. She really needed to get a life. Get out of the bubble where she'd been imprisoned. A strange analogy, considering she lived a fuller life—traveling around the country for competitions—than a lot of people would ever experience. At some point, her skiing could take her around the world.

"You're a grown woman. You should be able to make your own decisions, hang out with friends now and then." He hung his head. "I know there's more to it than that. I hope I didn't get you into trouble."

What an odd set of circumstances.

"Not your fault." She glanced up at the bright blue sky breaking through the evergreens and squinted. "I should probably just tell him. And if he asks me, I will. But he's busy. And Coach Hofler—"

"Look," Hudson interrupted her. "Let's just leave it for today, okay?" He didn't want to talk about the other coach. That conversation could yank them back from the new territory they were exploring in their relationship.

Shannon's gaze softened. She understood him. As always. And like no one else. Sometimes he wished he could just tell her everything, too. But not now.

If ever.

* * *

Shannon read a question in Hudson's eyes—did she understand?

"I hear you," she said.

He didn't want to talk about the only thing they'd ever had in common, because he wasn't happy with the way things had turned out. Neither was she. But maybe they could find more things in common as they got to know each other. She liked the idea. As much as she understood him, could read him well, she knew nothing about his personal life. When Daddy had mentioned that Hudson had issues, Shannon had brushed it off as an excuse, just another reason Daddy didn't want Hudson back at Ridgewood. But getting to know Hudson better might give her a glimpse into what Daddy was referring to.

Hudson slid his sunglasses down over his eyes. Too bad. In the intense sun and reflective snow, she could see tiny flecks of cerulean, making his eyes a brighter blue than usual. Making her heart skip. She didn't have long to think about it, because he started off again.

On the loop, they circled back and headed to the trailhead. She hated for their time together to end. Something new was building between them. Spending time with him like this made her almost forget how much she wanted him to coach her again.

She increased her pace to keep up with him. His hiking had morphed from a peaceful exploration of nature to something akin to a man on a quest.

"I've never seen this side of you."

"What side is that?"

"The 'hiking through the woods' nature-guy side." Okay. That sounded corny.

Hudson paused and turned to face her. Was he trying to decide if he'd made a mistake inviting her today?

She smiled to reassure him that he'd made the right decision. "I like it."

"There's more to life than racing," he said.

"You could be right." She recalled he'd told her that life wasn't a series of competitions.

He gaze was firm. "I *am* right."

Shannon couldn't breathe. This wasn't how she'd meant for things to turn out—she wanted to persuade him to come back and help her. Not lose sight of her own goal. But if anything, she'd done just that. She looked forward to a friendship with him that didn't revolve around downhill racing, which wasn't the plan. It seemed that Hudson was the one persuading her, getting her focus off her career.

Her thoughts had been on something else, all right—and he stood directly in front of her, his firm but gentle, striking eyes caressing hers. Persuading her, wooing her. Stealing her breath away. In that moment, she wanted to reach over and grab his hand. They were friends now, and she knew that he wanted to be more than just a coach. In his eyes, she saw purpose and much more. She saw the way he cared about her, and it was almost visceral, sending her pulse into the fall line of a downhill.

There was something much more than mere friendship between them. But her emotions tumbled, leaving her confused. Scared. She had to be wrong. She'd misunderstood what she'd seen and felt.

She sucked in crisp mountain air. "So what else have you got?"

There. She'd broken the spell.

His eyes widened. "What do you mean?"

"What else can we do in this life that's as awesome as racing down a mountain at breakneck speed?"

A chuckle burst through his big grin. She'd caught him off guard. He shook his head and scanned the surroundings, avoiding meeting her gaze this time, but he didn't answer.

"What's the matter?" she asked. "Cat got your tongue?"

When his gaze slid back to her, the intensity had returned. The strong emotions in his eyes were close to palpable again.

"You surprise me sometimes, that's all."

And you surprise me. She wasn't sure how she felt about whatever was happening between them, this new dynamic of their relationship. But she loved the grin on his face, and if Hudson the person was anything like Hudson the coach, she knew she was pretty fond of him.

"Well, what next, then?"

Hudson blew out a breath. "Shannon…" He released another sigh, making her nervous.

"Just say it," she said. He was about to tell her to go away and leave him alone. He was only being nice, inviting her along today. Whatever she'd read in his eyes she'd misconstrued.

Royally.

It was all she could do to keep a neutral face.

"I've enjoyed your company, but I want to be completely up-front. If you're spending time with me, believing that you're going to somehow convince me to come back and coach you, it's not going to happen."

He'd figured her out too easily. She should have expected that. He'd always been able to read her, except now he was wrong. She might have come with those intentions, but she wanted to be here with him, regardless.

"I understand. That's not why I came to see you before. That's not why I'm here today." She couldn't give up hope that he would coach her again, but there wasn't any point in hiding the full truth from him. "Okay. Maybe it was part of the reason on both counts. But I told you that I missed you and…I do."

They used to see each other almost every day. In the end, if he returned to coach her, that was merely a benefit of their renewed relationship. Apparently another benefit included spending a day outside of her world. This had been refreshing. Maybe it would give her a new perspective on life. After all, today she'd forgotten about the fall that had sent her off course.

"Glad we got that out into the open," he said, shoving the sunglasses onto his head. "But just remember that ulterior motives will get you nowhere."

Squinting, he studied her, caution in his eyes.

What was he afraid of? But then she remembered his earlier intensity. Was he afraid of getting hurt? Shannon reminded herself that he cared about all his students and friends. People. He was a compassionate and caring man. And that drew her to him.

A warm sensation enveloped her. Instinctively Shannon took a step forward. She almost reached for his hand but caught herself.

Looking down, she studied the snow she'd disturbed near her feet. "Thanks for inviting me along. I hope you can think of me as a friend instead of the girl you used to coach. I'll see you around."

But that wouldn't be true unless either of them went out of their way to make it happen. She took off for her Camry then. His words had twisted her emotions, and she needed time to figure them out.

"Shannon, wait."

Now it was her turn to play a game. Giggling, she started jogging. Just a little so she wouldn't aggravate her knee. Hofler wanted her in the gym for four hours this afternoon, and she was already late.

Snow crunched behind her as Hudson easily caught up. He grabbed her arm and she jerked away, pulling them both down, laughing. Thank goodness the soft snow cushioned their fall. Of course, falling from a snow jog was nothing like tumbling down the mountain when you were racing.

Their shared laughter finally died away, and Shannon gazed at Hudson, his face centimeters from hers. The guy was hard to resist. He was as sincere a person as she'd ever met, truly about others. His blue-eyed gaze caressed her face. She wanted to trace a finger down his rugged jaw.... Shannon gulped a breath.

She wanted to kiss him.

How insane, but there it was. Her breaths grew shallow as she envisioned her wish coming true. Hudson inching forward, pressing his lips against hers.

Did he read her well enough to know?

Just when she thought he would kiss her, he inched back, though he was still mere centimeters from her.

"I have an idea," he said.

No, he wouldn't kiss her today. But Shannon had a feeling the thought had entered his mind, too.

"What's that?" she asked, savoring his nearness.

"You could volunteer for the disabled-skiers program and work with me. Help me when you have time off." His gaze bored into hers, searching. "Then we'd see each other."

He had thought about *that,* when she had thought about kissing him? Disappointment settled in her stomach. She'd kind of hoped if he wanted to see her, he'd ask her to do something fun with him again like snowshoeing. If she turned him down, she knew that would hurt him because it would be as if she didn't value their friendship enough to make the effort.

"Well?"

She'd spent so much time and energy competing and nursing her own wounds, the idea of giving in that way scared her. "I'm not sure that I'm any good at that sort of thing."

Hudson reached over and toyed with a strand of her hair. Her lungs contracted. What was happening between them?

"Oh, the kids will love you," he said and released her hair. "You'll see."

Then it was over. He stood and offered his hand. Shannon allowed him to pull her to her clumsy snowshoed feet.

"What do you say?" He watched her. "You have a lot to offer."

"What? Are you on some sort of mission to show me what I've been missing in life?" She meant to tease him, but realized just how true those words had been.

"And what would be wrong with that?" He winked.

"I'll think about it." Shannon headed for her Camry.

Standing next to his Explorer, Hudson removed his snowshoes. "You'll do great. Helping others is like nothing you've ever experienced before."

With that comment, Shannon stood from removing her shoes to watch him over the hood of her car. "You know what? I believe you."

If it was that good for him, and it seemed to be, then Shannon wanted to share the experience, as well. Maybe... somehow, it would change everything that was wrong with her life.

But she knew that was wishing for too much.

When Hudson was waylaid by a phone call, she threw the snowshoes into the trunk. She'd have to return them today. She glanced at her watch and Hudson sent her an apologetic look. She couldn't wait around. Inside her car, she grabbed her cell, which she'd purposefully left behind.

She had a dozen or more text messages from her father and Cecile, who was simply telling her that her father was looking for her. She'd have to tell him, of course. What could he really have against her spending time with her former coach? Yeah, right. Time with him at her father's rival ski resort as a volunteer in the adaptive ski program was going to go over well. But it was the last text that made her muscles freeze up.

Hofler wanted to know why she wasn't at the gym.

Chapter 10

Hudson strolled into the Ender's Peak Ski Resort Café early enough to grab some grub before his afternoon of lessons with a new group of volunteer coaches started.

He drank in the surroundings of the great room and thought that no matter the surface differences, this resort was much the same as Ridgewood. His disabled students were different, too, but they were also the same as the Ridgewood Ski Team—some of the same dreams, drive, passion and motivation.

As he strolled toward the café that would soon grow crowded, he thought about the one big difference—Shannon wasn't here. He wouldn't see her during practice, training or rehab, or at the on-site gym. Nor would he run into her. This wasn't her father's lodge.

But now that she'd filled out the adaptive-ski-program application and gone through volunteer training, he would see her on occasion, depending on how often she chose to volunteer and work with him. That was, through the end of the ski season. It was already mid-March. Only a few more weeks of the season left in New Mexico.

He would see her this afternoon. Definitely something to look forward to.

Smiling, he sidled up to the counter and ordered coffee along with lunch from Clyde, a new friend at Ender's Peak. From across the room, Amanda made eye contact and headed straight for him. He took a sip from the quickly delivered mug while he waited on his order of jalapeño sliders and fries, and on Amanda's approach.

"Hudson, glad I caught you before you hit the slopes." Her dark eyes crinkled at the corners.

"What's up?"

"I've heard some great things about what you're doing out there. I knew you'd be a hit." She smiled.

"Thanks, I appreciate you letting me know."

"The thanks goes to you for making the change in your career. For making the move. We can always use good coaches." She slid onto a stool next to him. "People with heart."

Clyde set the plate of sliders on the counter in front of Hudson. He looked down. If she only knew his reasons. She might not think she had the right guy, after all. He was one of the guilty. He was to blame for causing someone else a life-altering injury. But Amanda didn't know that about him, and he was also guilty for keeping that well hidden. News of his sister's accident had been successfully shielded from the media years ago when it had happened.

"I'm glad you think so," he said.

"I do. And good job bringing Shannon de Croix on board as a volunteer for the disabled program. I know a lot of the kids really look up to her. She's such a great example of someone who doesn't give up. I hear she's still training hard for next season. Good for her."

Hudson tried to hide his consternation at the topic. With

his stomach growling and limited time to eat, he eyed his slider, but he didn't want to cut Amanda off. "Yeah, I think she'll be great with the kids." He hoped encouraging Shannon to become a volunteer hadn't been purely selfish on his part and that she would, in fact, be great with the kids. He knew she would be, though; he'd seen her with the little girl that day—she was a natural.

Amanda lingered but didn't order anything. Every time he was with her, he had the feeling she had more to say but held back. He wasn't exactly sure he wanted to hear more, anyway. Hudson decided if he was going to eat before his classes, it was now or never. He lifted a slider toward his mouth.

She drew in a deep breath. "So, you and Shannon, you're a couple, right?"

The meat fell out from between the slices of bun and back onto the plate. Hudson stared at her. "No. Why would you think that?"

She grinned, a twinkle in her eye. "Thought so."

"What are you talking about?"

"I won't lie. I sort of had my eye on you, but I can tell you're into that girl. Have you asked her on a date yet?"

Putting the disheveled slider back on his plate, Hudson let any thoughts of a hot meal go. What to make of this woman? She was bold, laying it out there. So…unprofessional to his way of thinking. There were always invisible lines drawn. But those things seemed to exist only in his fantasy world. Maybe those lines had become blurred because he'd ventured across them himself in his friendship with Shannon.

"I'm sorry." She laughed sweetly. "I've made you uncomfortable."

"A little." That was all he could manage.

She maintained the teasing glimmer in her eyes. He wouldn't tell her what she might want to hear—if he hadn't been into Shannon, he could see himself interested in her. Except after his part in Jen's accident, he couldn't pursue a woman in that way. How could he?

"Well, here's a suggestion." Amanda apparently wouldn't be deterred. "Have you thought about inviting her to the upcoming Flurry Fundraiser?" She nodded at the poster on the wall.

Why would Amanda think she needed to set Hudson up in a roundabout way? Play matchmaker, as it were, with someone he was already friends with? "No, I haven't thought about that. We're not… She's not… We're just friends." Why was he telling this love doctor anything? He didn't want her advice. She didn't know enough about him to give it.

But she was his boss and he had to be agreeable.

"Friends. For now…" She smiled and slid from the stool. She tugged something from her pocket and slapped it on the counter. "Two tickets to the fundraiser, compliments of Ender's Peak Ski Resort. Think about what I said. You're a good man, Hudson. A good coach, too. I want to keep you happy here."

An ulterior motive, then. Everyone seemed to have one these days.

He nodded, then she meandered over to bother some other unsuspecting person. Shoving his plate completely away, he scolded himself. He shouldn't think about her in such a negative way. She'd only been trying to help him, though he didn't appreciate her stepping so far into his personal affairs.

But she'd practically read his mind. Was he that transparent? He'd just been thinking that Shannon was the one missing ingredient and that he was glad he'd found a way to bring her here, even if just for a few hours every week. He slid the tickets across the counter and jammed them into his pocket. As the new director of the local disabled-skiers program, he hoped he wasn't expected to make some sort of speech, but then Amanda would have told him.

Two hours later, Hudson said goodbye to his last student for the day. The coaches' training had gone well, and then he'd assisted a volunteer with students. Frowning, he allowed his gaze to skim over the mountain streaked with ski runs and the resort and lodge below.

Shannon hadn't shown up. She'd already been through the volunteer training course. All that was required today was for her to assist him and another volunteer. He wouldn't leave her on her own until he knew she was ready. But it was a moot point if she didn't keep her work schedule, volunteer or not.

Disappointment roiled inside him. He should have known better—for her to break away from Ridgewood, from her rigid training schedule to assist disabled skiers, and from her coach and father, would be almost impossible.

He'd hoped she had found a way to work that out—it was for a good cause. No one could argue with that.

Or could they?

Carving through the snow on the downhill, Shannon concentrated on her position, her form and the slope ahead of her. But focus eluded her as she tried to shove thoughts of Hudson from her mind. Erase the image she conjured of his disappointed face when she didn't arrive for her volunteer session. It was impossible, though. With a heavy heart, she channeled her energy into finding the fall line and increasing her speed.

When Jason had left Ridgewood—due to a disagreement with Hofler, or more likely because he'd wanted to be head coach—her father had brought in Coach Bradford to replace him. Bradford's job was to focus on the star students. Travel with them to every race. Shannon hadn't thought anyone could be worse than Hofler, but she had been wrong.

After watching her a few times, Coach Bradford wanted more from her, claiming she wasn't putting everything into it.

Hudson had advised her to be patient. Maybe she'd finally surrendered to his instructions, only too late and for the wrong coach. If she didn't earn Bradford's respect today, she doubted he'd give her a break once a week to volunteer at another resort. He wouldn't believe she was serious about her career. And she'd been far too exhausted to work on her online classes.

She should have been grateful for a new coach who would focus more on individuals rather than the team at large. Someone new to help her get back on track. Considering that Coach Bradford had immediately focused in on Piper as if she had the potential he was looking for, Shannon was anything but happy.

In the wake of Shannon's accident, the girl had moved to the forefront of their team, seeming to outshine Shannon at every turn. Her father had gently nudged Coach Bradford's attention back to Shannon, emphasizing her need to train for the next season. But Piper was ready to race *now*.

Ignoring the never-ending pain in her knee, Shannon tucked deeper, becoming as aerodynamic as possible, knowing Coach Bradford observed her.

One last drill, he'd said.

That was two hours ago.

Her heart ached. The stunning realization hit her— for the first time she wanted to be somewhere else. She wanted to be with Hudson, assisting him with the disabled students.

When she'd explained that she'd made plans to volunteer on the afternoons she had free, Coach Bradford had

handed her the new training schedule. Hadn't she begged
Hudson for such a schedule?

"Your father says you're serious about your career."
Coach Bradford had raised his brows.

The man had no intention of taking her father's word
for it. She would have to prove to him that she was serious about her career. Serious about winning. This was the
chance she'd been hoping for, but now that the gate was
open, uncertainty threatened to waylay her.

Of course, she couldn't let her father down. Though
she *hoped* his love for her wasn't tied to her winning, it
appeared to be all that mattered to her father and these
coaches. To the ski team and the board. Even to Shannon.
Her life had been about competing in the downhill. If she
didn't excel, what did she have to offer? Her breakup with
Jack had certainly driven that point home.

Oh, Lord, what am I supposed to do?

Who was she if not a downhill racer?

The pressure to perform squeezed her chest.

But there was one person who saw things differently,
saw *her* differently.

Life isn't a series of competitions. Hudson's words always hovered at the edge of her thoughts.

Her new coaches' racing philosophies were diametrically opposed to Hudson's. The board had now completely
shifted away from Hudson's training techniques.

When she passed Coach Bradford on the sidelines, her
thoughts jarred to the moment. Pulse roaring in her ears,
cold biting her cheeks, Shannon focused on the imaginary
finish line at the end of the ski run.

She hoped Hudson would understand why she hadn't
shown up. If only Coach Bradford hadn't taken Hudson's place. If only Hudson remained her coach. With the
thought, a sliver of the hurt he'd caused by leaving her surfaced. His refusal to coach her could only mean he didn't

believe in her. In that way, he'd hurt her more than anyone. Maybe he wasn't different from the other coaches, after all.

Just as the unsettling considerations sank deep, she spotted him standing on the sidelines.

A spectator.

He could have been coaching her, but no, he watched instead.

Shannon continued to the end of the run, where she wedged her skis around to force a stop. When she glanced over to Coach Bradford to gauge his reaction, he was talking to Hudson. Now *she* was the one on the sidelines, watching the two of them shake hands.

She wasn't sure what to do now. Wait here and let the big boys talk? Or ski over and interrupt. When they swiveled their heads in her direction, she suspected they were discussing her.

She made up her mind.

Shannon skated her skis over to the coaches, past and present. Coach Bradford was midstory when she stopped, and he ended his tale with a chuckle. He reached over and squeezed Shannon's shoulder.

"I hear you're trying to steal one of my star students." He directed his words at Hudson.

Oh, so *now* she was a star student.

The grin slipped easily into Hudson's face, but Shannon caught the restrained frown between his brows.

"I told him I had to volunteer today, Hudson, but…" She pleaded with her eyes for him to understand.

"We all have to make our choices," Hudson said.

Not the response she'd wanted. His reply reminded her of his choice to leave Ridgewood.

"True enough," Coach Bradford said. "I made Shannon's choice for her this afternoon. If she's serious about getting back on track, she needs to work harder and longer."

"Volunteering with the disabled can help Shannon, too," Hudson said and smiled at her.

Her heart glided over the ice.

That Hudson had come here to check on her, that he was standing up to Coach Bradford for her... Warmth melted away her earlier traitorous thoughts. He did believe in her.

That meant everything.

Coach Bradford crossed his thick arms. "How so?"

Though she was curious to know the answer, too, watching the two sparring over one of their students was entertaining—to a point, considering that she was the student in question.

"If she doesn't have any time to herself, she'll burn out." Hudson was matter-of-fact.

Bradford's obnoxious chuckle seemed to echo in the mountains. "You're right. I just wanted to give you a hard time. And I wanted to see what kind of fire this girl has." His attention shifted to Shannon. "I'll tell you right here in front of your old coach that I think you can do this. Work hard enough and long enough and you'll get back in the race sooner rather than later."

Shannon had wanted to hear those words, craved them. Dreamed of hearing them from Hudson. But the words fell flat in her heart, falling to the frozen ground like a ski jumper landing well short of the goal. How could that be? Still, she'd earned Coach Bradford's respect, and she would use that to the full measure.

Hudson averted his gaze, but not before she'd seen the doubt in his eyes. He hadn't exactly said that helping others would help her career.

"Thank you, Coach Bradford," she said.

"I think I can give you an afternoon or two off during the week if you want to volunteer with Landers. That will give me more time with Piper." He grinned, his eyes leaving no doubt as to his intention. He meant to cut her with his words. Shrewd and manipulative, the man had given her the time off but at a price.

She didn't like him. What had Daddy been thinking? Maybe the choice hadn't been his. Maybe someone on the board wanted him in.

Coach Bradford turned his attention back to Hudson. "How's that sister of yours?"

Hudson had a sister? Any remnants of Hudson's smile disappeared, replaced by a disapproving frown. Though Shannon didn't know about his sister, by the look on his face, she sensed the sparring between the two had now turned brutal.

Chapter 11

Acid roiled in Hudson's gut.

Bradford sent Shannon up the slope again and then excused himself to take a call on his cell before Hudson could answer his question. Just as well. There'd been no sincerity. He'd simply meant to put Hudson in his place. He'd meant the question to be a gibe at Hudson's past. But to use his sister like that…

Hudson choked back the anger.

Bradford had been Hudson's own coach years ago, his and his sister's. Back then, Hudson had been a reckless skier, under Bradford's instruction. He'd been a daredevil, pushed himself to the edge, laughing in the face of danger. But he'd pushed too far when he'd dared to risk someone else's life. Hudson couldn't blame Bradford for the bad choices Hudson had made, but he'd give anything to have had a more cautious coach.

At least Hudson wasn't the same man now that he'd been back then. Far from it.

And Bradford knew the events that had ended Hudson's sister's career and caused Hudson to end his own. When Hudson came to Ridgewood looking for Shannon today, he'd been more than stunned to discover Bradford had been brought on board to coach Shannon and any others who showed accelerated potential.

Meeting him today and hearing his sarcastic tone at the mention of Hudson's sister drove the barbs deeper into his heart.

In his fifties, Bradford might have years of experience, first as a top skier himself and then as a coach, but that didn't mean he was the right one for Shannon. By leaving, Hudson had done this to her—but he hadn't had a choice, had he? He and Shannon were at odds on what was best for her career. He'd left so she would be free to pursue her dreams without him holding her back. Besides, when he was coach at Ridgewood, she wasn't supposed to be his only focus.

With the thought, he noticed a couple of his old students in the distance and waved. They walked toward him. Bradford cut them off and kept them there, and Hudson had no doubt that was on purpose. No matter— he'd come here against his better judgment to see Shannon. He should have let it go—she had to be the one to keep her commitment to volunteer. But he couldn't just leave it.

He glanced up the slope and caught her coming down, looking by all accounts as if she'd never taken that fall. She was definitely skiing at the top of her game today. But when she came to a halt at the end of the run, she pressed on toward the lodge and he almost lost sight of her in the gathering of skiers. She appeared to be in a hurry to escape, and he couldn't blame her.

If he was going to catch her, he'd better start hiking. But by the time he reached the building, she was already heading inside, lugging her skis over her shoulder and favoring her right leg.

But when she'd skied just now, he'd seen none of that. She appeared to have adapted.

Despite his displeasure at the whole situation, he couldn't help but smile at her tenacity. Except she shouldn't have to go to those lengths. Bradford shouldn't ignore that she'd been injured and still needed a few weeks before she could train hard without having to adapt.

When Hudson reached the door to the lodge, he hesitated. The chance of running into the wrong person was good, and that could result in unwanted conflict. He'd already had enough of that with Bradford, and he didn't want to cause Shannon more problems if she hadn't already mentioned the volunteer work to her father. Bradford would make sure he knew, of course, and might even insist he talk her out of it. In that case, speaking with her father—being up-front about his intentions—was the best thing. But he had to find Shannon first.

Hudson entered the lodge, and its warm familiarity comforted him. He missed this place, which had served as his second home for years. Cecile smiled at her customers at the counter where she served, and when she saw him, she waved.

Then Robert de Croix, Shannon's father, appeared at the end of the counter. Cecile immediately brightened, giving him a smile she'd reserved for him alone. Hudson knew that smile. He'd seen it on his sister's face when she'd look at her fiancé.

Glancing at Robert, Hudson saw Cecile's enthusiasm reflected in his face and smile, as well.

Good for them.

Did Shannon know there was something going on with her father and Cecile? The woman had been one of her closest confidantes, and a relationship with Shannon's father could completely change those dynamics.

Hudson made his way toward the man. When Robert saw him, he stiffened, his smile diminishing but not completely.

"Hudson, good to see you." He thrust his hand out. "What brings you here?"

Hudson shook the man's hand. "Stopped by to see a friend." Truth.

"Did you meet our newest addition to the coaching staff?"

"Bradford? Yes." Maybe Robert already knew that Bradford had once coached Hudson. In fact, why would Bradford leave that information out? But this probably wasn't the right time to bring up Hudson's opinion of the man, considering Robert's opinion of Hudson wasn't too great.

Before he discussed anything with her father, Hudson planned to talk to Shannon, to make sure she truly had an interest in volunteering and hadn't simply told him what he wanted to hear. He hoped she didn't think he'd intruded into her life by coming today.

"Everything going well at your new endeavor?" Robert angled his head.

Hudson thought he detected a hidden meaning behind his question. Was Robert really asking if Hudson wanted to come back so he could reply with a big fat rejection?

A person didn't quit on Robert de Croix. Even if moving on was best for everyone involved.

That was why Hudson understood much of Shannon's distress. If he hadn't already overstepped by showing up to see if she still planned to volunteer and by talking to her new coach, he was certainly about to overstep now. Though he'd wanted to talk with Shannon first, this was the time to speak with her father.

"I made the right decision. Love working with the dis-abled." Hudson ran his hand over his rough jaw. "Robert, you might already be aware, but I've asked Shannon to help me as a volunteer."

Truth—the whole of it. And at the look on Robert's face, Hudson should have allowed Shannon the privilege of sharing the news. She had a way with her father.

Hudson should listen to his own advice. He'd been im-patient.

"Not sure she'll have time for that. But I'll leave that to Bradford," Robert said.

He left Bradford to do the dirty work, keeping Shan-non from assisting Hudson if he wanted to, though in the end, it would have to be Shannon's choice. Would she have the strength to stand up to these two men if they chose to keep her from volunteering?

"Good enough," Hudson said. *Coward.*

He should have brought up that it was Shannon's choice, but again, she was a grown woman and he had already in-terfered too much.

When a Ridgewood employee approached Robert, he excused himself with the minimum etiquette required. Hudson exited the lodge before he could do more dam-age. Some friend he was. By coming here today, he had the feeling he'd just planted enough explosives to trigger an avalanche of repercussions for Shannon.

He was about to unlock his car when he heard footsteps approach from behind.

"Don't tell me you're leaving without saying goodbye?"

Grinning, Hudson turned to face Shannon and leaned against his Explorer. "I hadn't intended to leave before finding you, no. But I lost you in the crowd back there."

And he'd talked to her father. By the look on her face, she obviously hadn't seen them together. If she had, she'd be a lot more flustered at the moment.

Shannon averted her gaze, her eyelashes fluttering. Had she turned bashful on him? "I wanted to thank you for what you did back there. Standing up to Coach Bradford like that."

"I'm glad you feel that way. Was afraid you'd think I was interfering. When you didn't show up, I figured you'd gotten busy or weren't interested in volunteering. I needed to know."

"Of course I am. I told you I was. I went through the volunteer course. Jumped through the hoops."

"But you did all that without running things by your new coach, right?"

"He changed the schedule on me." She crossed her arms. "You two obviously know each other."

He hoped to avoid dredging up the past. For now. "Yeah. We go back a few years."

She lifted a brow, waiting for him to continue, but Hudson changed the subject. "Listen, you should know I mentioned that you would be volunteering to your father. I ran into him inside, and it just…came out."

"It just came out, did it? You seem pretty determined to get me over there. First you show up and have a word with my coach and then my father?"

Hudson held her gaze—he hadn't exactly untangled his thoughts on why he wanted her there. Too many reasons vied for first place and yet, deep down, he knew the biggest reason was both selfish and dangerous. Regardless, he wasn't ready to share any of them with her.

"I can't explain in words. You'll see why once you actually get involved." He grinned, hoping to defuse the detonation building inside her.

"How did my father react?"

"He left it to Bradford to make the tough decisions." Hudson figured that was one reason Robert had hired the man—he could be tough with his daughter where Robert couldn't.

"Right. And Coach Bradford wants me to prove to him that I'm worth his time. If I help you, no matter what he said about the schedule, he's going to think I'm not serious. Got any ideas?"

"Let me think." But instead of thinking about how to help her with Bradford, his thoughts went back to their snowshoeing day in the woods—how much he enjoyed spending time with her outside of this crazy competitive world of downhill racing. A world he wanted to escape. But a world he couldn't leave behind until Shannon no longer needed him there. He wanted to help her see life differently. He owed her that, considering his judgment call had changed everything for her.

If only he didn't want something much more with her than friendship. Hudson's sister had lost the use of her legs, and she'd lost her fiancé, because of Hudson. Nothing he did could ever make up for that, though he could try by giving back to others.

But how could he even entertain the idea of romance when Jen had lost so much? He didn't deserve to be happy after what he had done.

"Are you even listening?" Shannon asked. "How do I convince him that I'm serious?"

"I'm said I'm thinking."

Funny, hearing Shannon agonizing over convincing Bradford of her abilities. Her determination. Not so long ago, she was doing the same with Hudson. He should be glad her focus appeared to have shifted, but he wasn't. Maybe he felt a little too possessive, a little too protective where Shannon was concerned.

Then Amanda's words came back to him. She'd seen something between him and Shannon. Amanda had suggested he invite Shannon to the Flurry Fundraiser.

He hadn't considered it before. Not really. Should he or shouldn't he?

Shannon eyed him now, consternation written all over her face that Hudson didn't have an answer when suddenly, she flashed her smile. "Why are you looking at me like that?"

He grinned. "Listen, you want to go somewhere with me?" *Brilliant.*

"Um…right now? I can't. I have—"

"No, I meant…" Hudson scratched his jaw. "The Flurry Fundraiser. I'd love for you to go with me if you don't already have plans."

What was he doing?

A pretty shade of pink crept into her face. "You mean… No."

Hudson kept his shoulders high. He hadn't expected the rejection.

"Wait, I don't mean no, I can't go. What I mean is, yes, I'd love to go. I said no at first because I thought that, no, you couldn't mean on a date. I'd love to go with you." A nervous laugh escaped her.

Wait. What just happened? Was it a date or not? He wasn't even sure himself, considering her answer.

"Sounds good." Couldn't he think of something better to say?

Someone called Shannon's name and she glanced behind her. "Do me a favor, will you?"

"What's that?"

"Don't mention *this* to Daddy, okay? Let me be the one."

Hudson grinned. "Sure thing."

"What about the tickets? Aren't they expensive? Should I—"

"I have complimentary tickets for two." He grinned, feeling the tickets in his pocket as they spoke.

She backed away from him, a half grin dimpling her cheek. *Cute.* "See you next week to volunteer, okay?"

Promise? He knew she couldn't. "Okay."

She smiled—her beautiful smile that always lifted his spirits and warmed his heart—and hurried back to the lodge. He stared at the place, wondering about the circumstances and resulting decisions that had led him to leave Ridgewood. Thinking about the girl who'd kept him up at nights, and still, it didn't seem as if either of them were in a better place in their lives.

But next week, he would see her if she showed up to volunteer, and the week after that, he would attend the Flurry Fundraiser with Shannon de Croix on a pseudo-date. Guilt corded his throat. What about Jen? He opened the door to his Explorer and slid into the cold driver's seat. He needed to go see his sister. That would put everything back in perspective.

And that was what he was afraid of.

Standing on a green beginner's slope, Shannon assisted Hudson with a gorgeous little blonde-haired, blue-eyed girl named Cara who'd lost her leg.

Shannon wished she wasn't already exhausted. Her own legs quivered, and she prayed she could do what Hudson needed of her. Earlier that day, Coach Bradford decided he'd run her ragged, or rather ski her ragged. Was that because he knew she would volunteer that afternoon? She was beginning to loathe the man, and that wasn't the kind of relationship she wanted with her coach.

No time for slacking if you want to ski for me, he'd said to her and Piper, but his eyes had been on her, his words directed at her. She knew. Her goal of downhill-racing success had become convoluted.

When Cara smiled up at her, Shannon refocused her attention on the girl who needed her now.

"You can do this." Hudson winked.

She loved when he did that.

Shannon would assist Cara without Hudson's help this time. In his new job, he helped and assisted the skiers personally, as well as directed volunteers.

Cara's sweet angel face beamed up at her. "Don't worry, Miss Shannon. I trust you."

A pang shot through Shannon's heart. Cara counted on her. Hudson counted on her. They depended on her for something much different than winning a race. Something…more important to some. Maybe even to Shannon.

"Thank you, sweetie." Shannon returned Cara's smile.

In her peripheral vision, she could see Hudson's big grin. Her heart jumped, expressing a joy that she'd never experienced before. She wasn't sure what made her happier, Hudson's apparent approval or the little girl's delight.

Though Shannon thought she'd be nervous, she felt as if she could do anything with Hudson by her side, projecting confidence in her direction. Just like he had when he was her coach at Ridgewood.

She buried that reminder deep in the snow and focused on Cara again. Just before he left her on her own, Hudson caught her arm and leaned in.

"This will be her last run today. I need to check on some others. Meet me at the bottom of the slope when you're done." His foggy breath puffed around her.

"You're the boss." She grinned.

The warmth inflected in her words revealed how much he meant to her. Did he notice?

"I'm ready," Cara said, reminding Shannon that she waited.

Hudson nodded and stepped out of the way.

Cara skied forward and Shannon followed, gripping tethers attached to the bi-ski. Cara extended her legs as she sat in the chair with the two skis attached beneath.

She sliced through the snow like an expert on skis, the chair giving her as much freedom as her abilities allowed.

Cara's joy was almost tangible, or maybe that was Shannon's. She thought back to Hudson's words during volunteer training.

Downhill skiing rehabilitates the disabled in ways you can't imagine. Both physically and mentally. Their self-esteem grows, too, because they experience the same awe-inspiring exhilaration, the same freedom, as skiers without disabilities.

His words had inspired her that day and still lingered in her thoughts. He was right. This couldn't be expressed in words. It had to be *experienced*.

A sense of peace fell over Shannon as she followed gently behind Cara. She really could do this, just like Hudson had assured her. And he'd trusted her with a most precious person.

As they neared the end of the ski run, Shannon grew disappointed that her time with Cara would be over so soon. Shannon helped Cara slow and come to a stop. Another volunteer joined them and assisted Shannon, helping Cara out of the bi-ski. Cara's parents waved and smiled when they approached.

Cara looked at Shannon, sunlight shimmering in her blue eyes. "I had fun with you today, Shannon. Will you be here next time?"

"Of course, sweetie. I wouldn't miss it for the world." She smiled and squeezed Cara's hand.

Panic rose in her chest. What was she saying? How could she promise when her own obligations could very well stand in the way? Her ski coach could stand in her way. But this little girl had burrowed into her heart. She didn't want to let her down.

Hudson suddenly appeared next to the small group. "Cara, Shannon volunteers when she can, but she has a very tough coach training her. She's a downhill ski racer who has already won a lot of races."

Cara's eyes grew wide. "Oh, I want to do that. If I can do this, I can do anything."

"Keep practicing like you did today, and your parents may very well let you compete one day."

Cara's parents thanked Shannon and shook Hudson's hand. They were a warm and friendly couple, and they sounded pleased with the changes they'd seen in their daughter since she'd started the adaptive ski program.

When the small family left Shannon and Hudson, his eyes gleamed with admiration.

She couldn't get Cara's words out of her head. *If I can do this, I can do anything.*

"I get it," she said.

He smiled and nodded.

"I understand why you left coaching the ski-racing team to come here. This is rewarding, but in a completely different way. Maybe even a better way."

"God calls us to do different things." He studied her.

"What are you thinking?" she asked.

He gave a subtle head shake, then gazed off into the distance. "Nothing."

What? Was he hiding some deep dark secret? She reminded herself there was so much she didn't know about this man. A man she cared deeply about. He'd wanted to see her when she'd finished with Cara, and a small part of her wished he would ask her to dinner. Something. She very much wanted to get to know him better.

And not just because she wanted him to coach her. She smiled at the thought.

"You wanted to meet me, so here I am."

"You're right. I did. Just wanted to thank you for coming." Brooding, he toyed with his sunglasses. "What did you think about your first day?"

"Can we talk about this over a cup of coffee some-where warm?"

His brows drew together slightly. "I have another class, and you should probably get home so your father and coach will let you come back. I don't want to keep you too long."

She looked down, feeling the slight barb of rejection. He was right. She hated her lack of freedom and control over her own life.

"Hudson." She pinned him with her gaze, wanting to drive her point home. "Thank you for this. Thank you for what you did to get me here. This isn't something I can ever forget." She'd said those words to him before on the day he'd insisted they take the aerial tramway to the top. Hudson had a way of giving her experiences she'd always remember.

"And I hope to be back again soon," she continued. "I guess you could say I'm hooked."

"Good." A half grin put an end to his somber expres-sion.

What had brought on his subdued demeanor to begin with?

"See you later," she said. She started to ski over to a bench where she could sit and remove her skis, but Hud-son caught her arms.

"Wait," he said.

"Yes?"

He moved closer. "I'm glad you came. We're still on for the Flurry Fundraiser, right?"

Shannon wasn't much for playing games, but this seemed a good time to shovel a few of his own words, or rather similar words, back at him. "That depends. As a volunteer? A friend? What?"

His gaze searched hers, then roamed her face, impris-oning her breath in her lungs.

Then Hudson Landers took a step closer.

He lifted a strand of her hair. "I don't know. Maybe we'll talk about it then. That okay with you?"

"I guess it'll have to be."

His mood changes made her head and her heart spin. What would he do next? There was that feeling again. She wanted him to kiss her. She didn't care if it was right in front of everyone at the resort, though she doubted anyone cared.

Someone called Hudson's name and he released the lock of hair he'd been rubbing between his fingers. "I'll call you next week."

After removing her skis, Shannon loaded her gear in her car and headed home. He was right. She shouldn't spend too much time there with him, because she still had to answer to those who controlled her life and directed her career.

What was left of it. Initially, she'd thought by spending time with Hudson, she could somehow convince him how much she needed him to coach her again. Instead he was the one persuading her, by making her see the world differently, and she saw the importance of his work with the disabled to both him and the skiers in the program.

But she needed him, too, considering she struggled under Coach Bradford. She didn't know what the right answer was, but she knew she couldn't have it both ways. It didn't help that her feelings for Hudson were growing, because she couldn't have *him* both ways—as her coach and something more. Funny that she wanted to be valued as a person, rather than for her abilities as a downhill racer and the notoriety she could bring to her coaches and her father's lodge.

Unfortunately, she had a feeling that Hudson would really value her only if she didn't race at all.

Chapter 12

Shannon walked through the door of the cabin she shared with her father. The rich aroma of Italian cuisine filled the air.

"There's my girl," he said.

He slid a plate onto the table he was setting. What was the man up to? Shannon shrugged out of her coat and removed her boots.

"Okay, Daddy. What's going on? You don't cook." That was, unless he was trying to soften her up.

They generally ate at the café or went out to eat. Dinner at the cabin meant grabbing your own microwave meal or, in Shannon's case, a healthy smoothie or salad, especially during racing season. But she wasn't racing right now.

With the thought, her mood crashed, and she flung herself into the plush leather chair in the corner. A fire flamed in the potbellied stove.

"Can't I cook for my little girl on occasion?"

"It smells great." She was starved, although she'd eaten a protein bar an hour ago after she'd finished volunteering.

"Dinner's on," he said. "You want me to bring it to you?"

"No, I can make it to the table." She shoved to her feet.

Smiling at the lovely display, she sat down while he poured her a glass of water. That reminded her… "I saw you with Cecile today."

"Oh?" He dished spaghetti onto her plate and then his own. "She works for me, so that's not unusual."

"You know what I mean."

After his father said grace, she twirled spaghetti on her fork and snuck a glimpse at him. His reddened cheeks said it all. "You're holding out on me, Daddy."

For that matter, so was Cecile.

He stuffed his mouth and chewed.

Although Cecile hadn't mentioned anything to Shannon, maybe this was something new, and Shannon had been too busy training under Coach Bradford to notice. Something else she needed to bring up.

When Daddy finished chasing spaghetti with water, Shannon pressed his hand before he could take another bite. "Do you like her?"

"I do. She's a fine woman."

"Fair enough." Shannon couldn't help her grin.

Pressing the matter further might mess with a possible future her father could share with Cecile, she reasoned. She smiled to herself and ate in silence. Daddy deserved someone like Cecile, but on the other hand, she wasn't so sure Cecile would let him get away with his drive to excel. She'd often expressed her concerns for the way he pushed Shannon.

Best not to bring any of that up now. Let it work itself out. She hoped neither of them would get hurt.

"So how did the volunteering go today?" he asked.

Here we go. The real reason for the home-cooked meal. "What do you want to know?"

"How do they do things over there? Tell me about the resort. What did you see?"

"Not that you wouldn't already know most of this stuff, but I wasn't there to spy on them. I was on the slopes with Hudson and Cara."

"Hmm." Her father chewed, a disappointed look on his face.

She realized that was probably the only reason she'd been given the freedom to go. He and Bradford wanted to grill her about the competition.

"Well, then, tell me about volunteering with the disabled. I still can't believe Hudson left coaching a team of skiers who could go far for an endeavor that couldn't be nearly as rewarding."

If Daddy only knew. Shannon toyed with her food, hating to hear the disdain in his tone. "It's incredible. I've never experienced anything like it."

Which was more than pathetic. Hudson had opened her eyes to a lot of things about herself.

"What do you mean?" He'd stopped eating and stared at her. "There can't be anything that compares with what you do."

Shannon thought for a few moments. How did she explain? "Today was the first time I ever helped someone. My focus wasn't on me and working harder or becoming better or winning. My thoughts and energy were on helping a beautiful, precious little girl overcome her fears. Helping her to experience something I take for granted."

With the words, she realized just how much she'd taken for granted. Shannon leaned back in the chair and let the glow of that afternoon wrap around her once again.

"She said, 'If I can do this, I can do anything.' Imagine, Daddy!"

Hudson had a way with making people believe in themselves.

He'd done that for her, too, while he was her coach. He'd believed in her, made her believe in herself. Why hadn't she simply listened to him? Thinking about Hudson, she toyed with her fork.

Her father let his left hand drop to the table. Hard. Shannon jerked upright.

"See, this is exactly what I was afraid would happen." He shoved from the table, leaving his plate half full. "There's a need for people to help with that program. Don't get me wrong. But, Shannon, you have a different destiny and purpose. A different calling in your life."

Hudson had said something similar.

"You need to center your attention on what's required to get back on track in the downhill. So you fell. That happens. You get back up and you keep going."

"I am. What do you think I've been doing?"

He sat down again and eyed her. Finally, he slipped his hand across the table and covered hers. "You have a coach who is focused on you now. You don't want to take anything for granted? Then don't take *that* for granted. Everything I've built here, I've built for you."

She opened her mouth to protest, but her determined father held up his hand.

"I have given my life for you. Put everything into giving you what you needed to make this happen. It's what you wanted."

Tears pounded the back of her eyes. "You're right. It's what I wanted. But don't tell me you didn't want it, too."

"Of course I want you to race—to win, too."

If she wanted his affection, that was exactly what she'd have to do. And she hated that. Shannon fought the need to leave him at the table.

"All I want is for you to be happy," he said.

Finally the tears slid down her cheeks. She swiped them away and sat taller. "Maybe racing is not what I want anymore."

Had she just said that?

She couldn't stand the hurt in his eyes. He looked as if she'd just slapped him. Shannon left the table and fled to her room. She flung herself onto her bed and sobbed into her pillow as if she were a child.

Maybe her father was right. If she hadn't volunteered, done a good deed, then she'd be focused on her goal of getting her racing game back on. That was what she wanted, wasn't it? What she'd always wanted? She rolled over and stared at the ceiling.

No.

What she wanted was for Daddy to be proud of her no matter what choices she made. For him to approve of her life even if she didn't win another race. But this life was all she knew—it was her identity. She wasn't sure she could stand to be around herself if she didn't excel at the one thing she was good at.

If I can do this, I can do anything.

What would it take for her to believe in herself like that again?

Hudson.

A soft knock drew her up. She should just get her own apartment, but she and Daddy, they had only each other. "Come in."

Her father pushed the door open. "I'm sorry. I just don't want you to miss your chance, that's all. You're already twenty-two."

Her father's past regrets clouded his vision for her future.

"I know," she whispered.

"What you do is your decision," he said. However, she

saw the truth in the deep set of his eyes. He still counted on her to succeed for the both of them.

The air seemed thinner on his mother's front porch, though Hudson knew that couldn't be the case. The altitude in Dallas, Texas, was just over four hundred feet. His New Mexico high-desert playground was thousands of feet more. Of course, the elevation had nothing at all to do with his struggle to breathe. If he hadn't already touched the doorbell, he might have changed his mind and left despite the fact he'd taken a couple of days off to make the trip.

The door swung open much too soon.

His mother gave him a smile that only a mother could give. "You know you don't have to knock. Come on in."

Hudson entered the foyer of the North Dallas home where his parents had moved with Jen after they'd grown tired of the snow. Why endure the cold weather and the nasty sludge that snow eventually became? After all, Hudson had stopped competing, and Jen was in a wheelchair.

He continued into the living room. His mother had changed colors again since the last time he'd been here, everything now in matching hues of sage. He dropped his carry-on luggage to the floor.

"Let me put that in your room." His mother always kept a room for him in case he came for a visit, but that wasn't often enough for her, he knew.

He tugged his stuff back. "No, I've got it. Thanks, Mom."

She paused to really look at him. "I'm so glad you came."

"It's good to be here." He hugged her quickly. "You're looking well."

"Thanks. I'm cooking a roast for supper. Your favorite."

"Thanks. I don't get that too often these days."

"No. I don't suppose you do." She arched a brow. His

mother thought he needed a good wife by his side. He knew it would come up at some point, and he didn't want to hear it now.

"Is Jen around?" He thought she'd be home from her job at the architectural firm by now.

As if in answer to his question, Jen rolled into the living room in her wheelchair. Pain squeezed his insides. Pain and guilt that he'd never get over, and why should he? Jen was certainly confined to the fate he'd given her. She was such a beautiful girl, and she'd been engaged. Hudson's mistake had cost her everything.

It should have been him in the wheelchair. Not lovely Jen.

"Hudson!" Her smile beamed.

And she was still beautiful.

She rolled forward and reached for him.

Swallowing past the lump in his throat, he grabbed her hand. He missed Jen so much. Missed seeing her out on the slopes with him. But she was in Texas now, and not of her own choice. He could hardly wait to tell her he was working with an adaptive ski program. Would she want to come to New Mexico with him and ski again?

She squeezed his hand, her face full of love for him. He saw no resentment in her eyes whatsoever. She'd found a way to forgive him and move on. The resentment and bitterness were his alone, and he hoped she couldn't see that he still carried the blame around with him.

"Supper will be on soon." His mother carted his luggage away down the hall, and he let her this time. "I'll just put this away in your room. You do remember where that is, don't you?"

He had to concede that he'd acted the stranger. "Sure, Mom. Thanks."

Jen rolled around the blue leather sofa that sectioned off the living room. "Have a seat. Let's talk. I want to

hear all about your racing team. How's that girl...what's
her name...Sha—"

"Shannon." He scraped a hand down his face. This was
going to be a long evening. "Her name is Shannon."

The fact that Shannon's name was the first one off Jen's
lips revealed something. He must have talked about her a
lot the last time he'd been home. Truth time. He'd had a
thing for Shannon far too long. There were other talented
skiers on the team. There was Piper. But Hudson could
see only Shannon.

The aroma of Mom's roast filled the room, making his
stomach rumble. He plopped onto the sofa, feeling the
weariness to his bones. Like he'd aged ten years.

"You remember she fell during the first race of the season, right?" he asked.

Jen frowned. "How's she doing? She going to be able
to come back?"

Hudson pressed deeper into the sofa. "It's complicated."

"Oh, I'm sorry to hear that. She had so much potential."

How could Jen sit there and talk about Shannon's potential when she herself had had potential? She was Hudson's sister. She'd won her own races, had been making
her own name when she'd fallen.

"And still does. She could make a comeback, if she
would slow things down long enough to heal completely."

"But she's not listening to you? What about her sports
therapist? Her doctor? What do they say?"

Hudson clasped his hands over his head. "No one else
sees anything wrong. Nothing on the MRI. She doesn't tell
them about the pain. She hides it from everyone."

Jen's eyes filled with understanding. "But *you* know.
You see it."

Hudson nodded. "I'm her coach. I work with her every
day." He *was* Shannon's coach. He had worked with her

every day. But he wouldn't get ahead of himself yet. He'd tell Jen everything soon enough.

How could he read Shannon so well? Was it his years of experience? Or was it because he was in tune with Shannon?

"Why? Why would she want to push herself like that?" Jen asked.

He knew all too well why. The competition was stiff. People made demands on her. "Listen, Jen, I didn't come to talk about Shannon."

She studied him. "What's going on?"

"I don't teach the ski team anymore. I left Ridgewood to work with a disabled-skiers program at another resort."

"You what?" Jen and his mother—who'd apparently stepped into the room at that moment—asked the question simultaneously.

Jen shifted in her wheelchair. "Hudson…that's incredible."

Her enthusiasm inspired him. He sat forward, eager to tell her everything. "I can't tell you how good it feels. It's like I'm really making a difference."

"And you don't think you were making a difference with the ski team?" she asked.

His sister knew him too well. She could see right through him, right through his euphoria at his new job and what it meant. He should have moved on a long time ago, but there was more to it and Jen knew it.

A little quirk crept into her mouth. "Am I digging too deep?"

"A little."

"This wouldn't have anything to do with Shannon, would it?"

Everything to do with her, and with you, Jen. "What makes you say that?"

"Ah, so you're not denying it." Jen smiled.

Hudson didn't respond, still searching for how to explain. He hadn't even figured things out himself.

"It's just that," she said, hesitating, "you seem a little enamored with her. I just thought maybe she had something to do with the reason you left. Either her, or..." Jen stared at her hands. "Hudson, you're not doing this because...because of me, are you?"

"Does the reason matter?"

Jen held out her hand, and Hudson took it. "I don't blame you for what happened. I never did. You need to stop blaming yourself."

How could he? "I thought you would like to come out sometime and ski with me." Maybe it wouldn't be like old times, but it would be something.

"Sure, I'd love that. My job is here, though, and...this seems like a good time to tell you that I've met someone."

He hoped he imagined the moisture in his eyes. He didn't want Jen to misunderstand or cause her more concern. "That's wonderful."

Her brilliant smile said everything.

He'd tried to deny himself that kind of relationship for so long, and he'd struggled with his feelings for Shannon, and all because of Jen. Guilt threaded his heart to think that he'd let himself care about Shannon despite his resolve.

But Jen's news was good. This wasn't about him. It was about her. "So when do I get to meet this someone special?"

"Supper's ready." His mother interrupted their discussion. She leaned into the living room from the kitchen. She'd obviously gone back to preparing their meal at some point during the conversation. "Your father's going to be late, and he said we could go ahead and get started."

Jen backed up. Just before she passed Hudson, she grabbed his hand. "So what about Shannon? What's standing in your way?"

"A lot." But maybe one less thing. Winning would always be too important. Hearing that Jen had romance in her life again, seeing how great she was doing, should have been a freeing experience, but instead he felt the blame more keenly.

Chapter 13

In the chapel in New Mexico where he attended worship services, Hudson sat in a pew and tried to listen to the sermon. He was off track. Way off, and he needed to get back to the fall line—to get centered once again.

He held his Bible between his hands and then let it flip open, unconcerned about the specific passage Pastor Hank read from.

"'There is therefore now no condemnation…'"

Hudson had heard all that. He knew that. Believed it to his core. But it didn't make a difference. He'd made a serious error in judgment that had permanently hurt someone he loved dearly. How could he *ever* get over that?

The sermon over and services dismissed, Hudson stayed in the pew, pressed there by his heavy heart. He'd thought seeing Jen would help him, but even though she was thriving, his visit was having the opposite effect.

A hand gripped his shoulder, and irritation zipped through him. Couldn't he just be left alone? He gazed up to see Pastor Hank smiling at him. Hudson had attended the small chapel for the past three years, but had never hung around long enough to meet the man, always choosing to duck out a little early. The man might ask too many questions.

Pastor Hank thrust his hand out. "Good seeing you here today."

"Thanks." *Now just move along, please.*

"God's grace is sufficient, son. If it wasn't, we'd all be in trouble. His grace is all you need."

Hudson couldn't help his somber expression, and he nodded. Fortunately, Pastor Hank left him to his thoughts and went to chat with other parishioners who lingered. Hudson grappled with the man's words. Somehow they seemed to be just what he needed to hear—zinging right to his heart.

How had the man known what to say? Hudson shouldn't have to ask—Pastor Hank's words meant that God was listening. God heard Hudson's anguish, and He had the answer for it. Either God's grace was sufficient to cover even the worst evil committed by humans on the earth, or it wasn't. All Hudson had to do was accept it.

Why was that so hard?

Hudson was anything but comfortable in the monkey suit, but at least the Flurry Fundraiser event was semi-formal and he didn't have to rent a tux. He paced outside the Eldorado Hotel, where the event was being held, while he waited for Shannon. She had suggested they meet there.

No knocking on her door, picking her up as if it was a normal date. A *real* date. But he hadn't known exactly what this was supposed to be. He'd told her they would talk about it tonight. However, now it seemed a little crazy going into this without a clue.

Though it was the end of March, the temperature was

in the thirties tonight, even at Santa Fe's lower elevation. He jammed his hands into his pockets to keep them warm. Nothing like waiting outside in the cold without a coat, but his ski jacket sort of messed with the whole look. This would probably be a once-in-a-lifetime moment. Or at least once a year, at this annual event.

Thinking about all the ski bums dressing up for an evening of dining and who knew what else made him grin. All for a good cause, of course—to raise funds for the disabled-skiers program. Important people would be here tonight and those in the community who wanted to help by giving. Thank goodness he would only be introduced as the new director and nothing more would be required of him. The evening had been planned well in advance and before he came aboard—but next year, Amanda had warned him, next year he might have to get up and say something. Hudson hadn't exactly considered that aspect of the position, but if he had time to prepare, he would do anything for the disabled-skiers program.

Lost in the uncomfortable thoughts, Hudson spotted the mayor and his wife, parking their car. Hudson stepped back into the shadows, preferring to be a wallflower as long as he could, at least at social events of this caliber. *Coward.*

A few more cars, including Shannon's Camry, crunched over the parking lot. Hudson's palms slicked—he'd wanted to invite her to this. Or had he? Amanda had planted the seed and he'd allowed it to take root. But since his trip to Texas to see Jen and his parents, he was more confused than ever.

When Shannon stepped from her car, she struggled with her dress. Hudson started toward her to help, but then she headed his way. Thank goodness she wore a warm wrap.

As Shannon approached the hotel, she searched the entrance. Her gaze landed on him and she smiled, hurrying across the parking lot as best she could in dainty shoes that matched her dress. His pulse raced at the sight of her, at her dazzling smile.

He returned it with a grin of his own as she drew near.

Finally she stood next to him. "Thanks for agreeing to meet me here."

"You didn't want your father and me to have a confrontation. I get it." He held his elbow out for her. "Shall we?"

She slipped her arm through, which warmed him as well as any insulated ski jacket. Once inside the Eldorado, they found two places at a dining table. The room quickly filled to its capacity of a few hundred. Hudson assisted Shannon with her wrap. Her gorgeous tresses were pinned on her head, allowing him to see her long, graceful neck.

Shannon remained standing, her eyes roaming over him. "You clean up real nice."

Hudson took in the elegant lavender silk that draped her slim but athletic frame. He'd never seen her dressed in anything except skiwear. His heart skipped erratically.

So beautiful, so feminine and...was it for him?

No, everyone had dressed up for the occasion.

The thought tempered his mounting emotions. He lifted his hand to touch a small curl hugging the creamy skin of her cheek. He rubbed it between his fingers, feeling the silkiness, like he'd done on the slopes not too long ago. He loved touching her hair.

"And you...you take my breath away." Please. No. He did not just say that.

Her cheeks coloring pink, she glanced away, then back to him. "I hoped you would like it."

So she *had* dressed up for him. He didn't know what he was doing. He wasn't ready for this, to take this step with her or anyone. He'd kept himself in chains for so long that freedom—if he really deserved the freedom to love—was difficult to navigate.

But Shannon was waiting for him to show himself the

gentleman, and now wasn't the time to figure things out. Hudson assisted Shannon into her chair. He had a full evening ahead with her, and they wouldn't be alone. Six other people had already taken their seats at the round table, just one of many tables, and even more fundraiser attendees were arriving. All good. The disabled-skiers program needed everything the community could give, including time, hence the volunteer coaches.

A lean man in his forties took the dais and introduced himself as Chuck Samson. He began the typical welcome speech and introductions—including introducing Hudson as the new director, for which Hudson had to stand—then gave permission for the attendees to enjoy their dinner. At some point, there would be a slideshow and a keynote speaker presenting compelling reasons ski programs for the disabled were of value. Hudson would pay close attention in order to prepare for whatever his role would be next year.

The waiters busied themselves bringing salads to every table. Shannon's hand rested against the white tablecloth. He wasn't accustomed to seeing her hands because they were always in gloves. Unwilling to hold back, Hudson slid his hand over hers. Suddenly he wished that their first date—if she was thinking along those terms as well, because he certainly was now—could have been somewhere else.

He wished they could have been alone so they could talk.

Her hand felt small, warm and so soft beneath his. He never dreamed that he would be sitting here with her like this. As right as it felt, there was something equally not right about it.

When a salad was placed before everyone at the table, Hudson released her hand and fumbled with his fork instead.

* * *

Shannon toyed with her baby-arugula salad. Salads were so hard to eat—lettuce so clumsy, falling everywhere or sticking in her teeth. The man sitting on Hudson's other side had engaged him in conversation, leaving Shannon to her thoughts.

She'd had a row with Daddy today about attending tonight. Again with the focus.

And he would be right. Her skiing was off. Way off. She told Daddy she didn't know if she could tolerate Coach Bradford any longer. She didn't want to talk about any of that tonight, though. She was here with Hudson—the man she'd idolized in her early teen years.

Then when he'd come to Ridgewood to coach, Shannon had really taken off on the skis, more so than before. She couldn't understand how her father had so easily let him go. But then Shannon had been the one to brush aside Hudson's advice.

She still didn't understand how Hudson had been so affected by her slightly rebellious spirit that he'd left Ridgewood, even though she'd witnessed his abilities with the adaptive ski program.

But he was here now beside her, though not as her coach.

Her hand still tingled from when he'd covered it with his own sturdy hand. She sipped her tea and found Hudson watching her. His eyes, the muted dusky blue of snow in the full moon, stared back.

Her heart fluttered, and she could swear her eyes did, too. So was she right in assuming this was a date, after all? She hadn't been completely sure.

"Hudson…I…"

"Shannon…I…"

They'd spoken in unison and laughed together.

"You go first," he said.

"It's nothing. I'm just glad you invited me here, that's all."

"Thank you for coming."

"I missed you last week. I showed up to volunteer. They said you were in Texas."

His face twisted into an awkward smile. "I'm sorry about that. Had to go see my family."

The waitstaff removed the salads and delivered plates decorated in New Mexico cuisine. Chicken breast, yellow beets, mole rapido and southwestern-style potatoes. Shannon picked up her fork, but nervous energy had zapped her appetite. "I'd really like to know about your family."

Then she remembered when Coach Bradford had asked him about his sister. She had meant to find out more if she'd had time, but her life had not been her own. She'd been fortunate to escape for tonight.

He grabbed his tea and took a swig, eyeing her over the rim. He paused long enough that Shannon began to think he didn't want to talk about his family.

The woman sitting next to her brushed her arm, and Shannon turned to face her.

"Hi, I'm Hillary Swann."

Smiling, Shannon introduced herself, then spent the next half hour in conversation. She'd have preferred talking to Hudson, but she couldn't be rude and knew it was best to engage.

Hillary's husband drew his wife's attention from Shannon. Shannon hadn't touched much of the main meal, but she eagerly finished her chocolate cheesecake, more like relished it.

When Hudson concluded his conversation with his neighbor, he turned back to Shannon.

"So," he said, "how did it go when you volunteered? You know, the day I wasn't there."

"I had Cara again. What can I say?" She wrapped her

mouth around the last piece of cheesecake and smiled at him.

"You don't have to say anything. I can read it on your face." The way he gazed at her, tingles ran over her skin. He seemed to know her so well.

"After this party is over, can we go somewhere private?" she asked. "I want to talk. Just the two of us." *And...*her throat grew tight...*I'd really like to run my fingers through that thick, dark hair of yours.*

Where had that thought come from? She couldn't deny that maybe it had been there inside her for a while now. It didn't matter, though. She doubted she would have that chance tonight. They weren't that close yet. If they ever would be. Nor was she even sure she should pursue this... whatever it was. Infatuation? No. She'd been infatuated with Jack. They'd had everything in common. They'd been making waves in the ski world together. Until she'd fallen.

This was something much more.

But thinking of Jack made her think about Hudson quitting on her. How could she get him back?

Two hours later Shannon was warm and cozy in Hudson's Explorer.

He glanced at her, smiling as he drove, his hand placed over hers on the console. They had a kind of happy silence between them—just enjoying the warm chemistry of being together. That was her perspective, at least.

"Are you sure you don't want to change into something else?" he asked.

"Are you kidding? I go home now and Daddy won't let me leave. Doesn't matter my age."

"Okay. Well, the Waffle House might think it's prom night." Hudson turned into the parking lot. "But they stay open late, so we can talk as long as you want."

"Are you sure you're ready for that?" She laughed.

He turned off the ignition and looked at her. "Or we can sit right here. Just the two of us."

Drawn to him, Shannon leaned closer. "Mmm. I'd like that."

"I'll turn it back on if we start to get cold. But I feel pretty warm right now. You?" His face was close now, and her heart threaded at a frantic pace up her neck and then down her belly. His gaze roamed her face as if he was soaking it in. As if he hadn't seen her a thousand times over the past four years. Her breath hitched.

"Shannon," he said, his voice a husky whisper.

He lifted his hand and slid it behind her neck, urging her gently forward. As if in a dream, Shannon floated along on the moment as Hudson drew closer, his breath fanning her cheeks. She thought he'd never kiss her, but it seemed he was luxuriating in the moment. Their closeness. They knew each other—something inside connected—and they were drawn to each other.

Finally, slowly, he pressed his lips against hers. Softly, at first, then deeper. Shannon shifted in the seat to get closer to him. She'd wanted this…for so long.

Hudson eased away until his lips were barely touching hers. They breathed in and out together, wanting to stay connected.

"I didn't know," she whispered.

Their foreheads pressed together, she opened her eyes to see his smile.

"How could you?" he asked.

Just how long had he had a thing for her?

"Why didn't you tell me?" she asked.

"How could I?"

She eased away a little and kept a teasing grin in place. "Okay, enough with answering my questions with a question. How long, Hudson?" Did she really want to press him on this?

He pulled away, a frown edging into his brows.

"I'm sorry. It doesn't matter. It's enough to be with you." There. That should ease his tension. Why had she pressed him?

"No, it's okay," he said. "Awhile, actually."

Shannon sat up. "Please don't tell me you quit coaching me because…"

Hudson leaned all the way against his door now. He'd put as much space as he could between them. She would bet that any minute he would start his Explorer and drive her to her own car. If she could take it all back, she would, but she had to know.

"No. Maybe," he said. "No. That was only part of the reason."

Shannon reached for his hand. "Please, Hudson, if you care anything about me, I need you to come back and be my coach. You have no idea what it's like. I can't take this anymore."

"You don't need me. You don't need Bradford, either. What you need, if you're serious, is to head somewhere you have a whole team of coaches and sports scientists available."

"I have to achieve a certain level for that, and you know it. And that would mean leaving Daddy." She stared out her own window, watching the patrons inside the Waffle House. "And you. All I need is you to coach me. I don't understand you." This time the tears coiled in her throat.

Hudson eased his hand away and started the Explorer.

She didn't understand herself.

Chapter 14

At Ender's Peak Ski Resort, Hudson rode the Gold Coin Chairlift to the drop-off point, then skied over to ride the Eagle's Chair, which was the highest lift at the resort. The lift closed at one o'clock, and he'd taken the afternoon off. To get to the very top of the mountain, which loomed over twelve thousand feet, he'd have to hike his way along the ridge, and that would take almost an hour.

At that point he'd be above the tree line, and he could enjoy the most spectacular views along with his choice of any number of chutes and chokes. Black-diamond country. And up here, first tracks were easier to catch.

The ski lift took him higher until the evergreens, heavy with snow, began to thin out.

At the launch point, he eased from the chair and skied forward. Once he was well out of the way of the next chair, he stopped to take in the magnificent view. Before starting his trek toward the ridge that would take him to the top, he removed his skis and placed them over his shoulder.

Hudson hiked past the ski-patrol headquarters. Ender's Peak was a Class A resort, meaning an avalanche could occur at any time and place, but the ski patrol used control measures to keep the resort boundaries safe for skiers.

Finally, he reached the ridge of the mountain where he could see the snow-covered Sangre de Cristo Mountains in every direction.

Time alone. A big-picture perspective. And the perfect bluebird day.

That was all he needed to get his thoughts straight regarding Shannon. A girl who'd gotten under his skin in a big way. She'd shaken up his life. His decision to leave her ski career in someone else's hands had seriously affected her, too. It wasn't looking all that positive, either. For that, he was sorry.

He'd come up here searching for clarity.

Only a couple of others dared to join him on the ridge today—it was the middle of the week and the resort was devoid of the weekend ski traffic. Hudson continued his hike to the peak, looking forward to the rigorous exercise he would experience today.

The kiss he'd shared with Shannon wouldn't leave his thoughts. The memory surfaced full force, and it rocked him. He was going crazy. Had no idea if the kiss had been real for her. If the date had been real for her. The way she'd looked at him, acted around him, had any of it been real?

How could he trust what had happened between them when in the end, all she'd seemed to want was for him to come back and coach her?

Why couldn't she just move on?

For that matter, why couldn't he? He was a genuine coward for refusing to help her.

In the distance, he spotted a couple of hikers behind him along the ridge, but he'd been the one to make the first tracks today. That was his cue to get going. He'd wanted the mountaintop, the run, all to himself.

He finally made it to the peak, where he eyed the highest ski run at the resort—Excelsior, which meant "ever upward." Closing his eyes, he drew in a breath of cold, clean mountain air.

One of the skiers along the ridge called out something. Annoying. He'd wanted to be alone, but that was obviously asking too much. Skiing Excelsior would likely mean he'd be joined by the other two skiers, as well.

Hudson had two choices. Excelsior or a mountain trail less traveled.

Hudson hiked around to Roulette, the name backcountry skiers had given the ski run that was on the out-of-bounds side of the mountain. After Jen's accident, he'd made an effort to ski safe and put away his reckless ways for everyone's sake.

His whole body tensed—by doing this, he would cross a line he hadn't crossed in years. At least he'd worn an avalanche beacon to ski Excelsior in case the worst happened. He stared down the mountain, giving it some thought. If he really wanted perspective, what he needed right now was something that would remind him of the man he used to be.

So this was it, then.

He shoved off, feeling the risk he took to his marrow, gut-wrenching and visceral. It was exactly what he needed.

The crisp March day, piles of powder... He'd almost forgotten the bliss this kind of skiing could bring. Still, the danger tempered his pleasure, and yet it was the danger that brought clarity to everything wrong with his life.

Caution breaking through, he slowed when he made the tree line and skied from tree to tree, then paused to catch his breath. Looking back, he spotted another skier on Roulette.

No, no, no...

This crazy risk had been for him alone.

The skier carved through the powder along Hudson's path.

And skied right to him. Her skis parallel, she turned her body into a hockey stop, scratching into the snow and showering Hudson.

That was cutting it too close.

He opened his mouth to give her a few words when she tugged off her helmet. Auburn hair tumbled over her shoulders. Bright eyes squinted in the sunshine, accented by the world's greatest smile.

Stunned to see Shannon, it took him a second to recover. He'd needed this time alone to gather his thoughts about the girl in front of him. So he wasn't exactly sure how he felt that she'd joined him in the danger zone.

What was she doing? More important, "How did you find me?"

He realized she'd been the skier on the ridge.

She smirked a grin. "Amanda. You've got a friend in her."

Yeah, he knew. And more, if he were interested. Amanda would be a much better fit for him than Shannon. But Shannon made him feel...

Alive.

Like this backcountry run.

She was dangerous, unchartered territory.

"She said you'd mentioned Excelsior. But...*Roulette?* I'm a little intimidated by this."

"Then why'd you follow me?"

"I'd follow you anywhere." Teasing, she smiled sweetly.

But those words echoed, a haunting reminder of Jen. Her exact words.

Lord, please help me....

He had to get her to safety.

He scanned the slope below them. The pitch was gradual on this side, and more open space until the rocks. "There are some big drops. You sure you're ready for this?"

"I won't take it too fast."

"Sometimes that's not a choice."

"Yeah, well, considering I'm here, there's nothing else to do besides ski down."

He'd meant the slope, but his thoughts hinged on their relationship. He'd been in too deep for far too long, and now that Shannon was into him, things weren't just one-sided; things were moving along much too fast. Like neither of them had any control over it. That was, if Shannon wasn't just playing him to get what she wanted: him coaching her again.

"I know," he said. At least until they could cross back over into the resort boundaries.

Silence reigned, clinging to the powder and mountain and clouds. Dangling between comfortable and awkward.

"I'm skiing more these days. Getting back up to speed. The knee is getting better, though it still bothers me sometimes."

Then Bradford's training was working for her. "You mean the knee you'd never admit to anyone bothered you?"

She smiled. "That'd be the one."

Again the silence. But more comfortable now.

"As soon as we can, let's cut across and back into the groomed trails, okay? You shouldn't be here." Neither should he, and he hated that he'd put her in danger. But at least this was more of a side-country ski run—it wasn't too far from the ski-resort boundaries.

"Hudson…I shouldn't have come today. If you want to be alone…"

The anxiety he saw on her face was too much and he finally relented, revealing a teasing grin. "I'm glad to see you, just not…here."

"I thought… I shouldn't have asked you to coach me again. I'm sorry. Can we just forget it?"

More than anything, he wanted to forget. He couldn't blame her for asking, but he wanted to know how she really felt about him, and yet he still wasn't sure he should take that path with her.

"I don't think it will be that easy."

"I understand." She adjusted her helmet back on her head. "Listen, I had a really nice time with you at the fundraiser." She averted her gaze. Afraid of what she might see in his eyes?

She was trying to tell him what he wanted to hear.

And he was being such a jerk. Holding back. He wanted to let go. Be free. Give her everything he had to offer. *God, help me*….

"I did, too," he finally said. *You have no idea how much.*

"Maybe we can do it again sometime?" Her smile grew shy.

"It's a once-a-year thing." Now he toyed with her. She had trekked all the way out here to find him, and he was giving her a seriously hard time.

"Okay. Well. Now I'm starting to feel like a fool for coming to find you, so I'm just going to go now. Catch me if you can."

Then Shannon pushed away from him and headed down the ungroomed and unpatrolled mountain.

"Shannon! Wait!" Hudson called from behind.

She wasn't about to stop. He'd have to chase her down the mountain if he wanted to talk to her. She angled her head enough to spot him in her peripheral vision. Why was he acting so distant?

Maybe he just wanted to protect himself, but from what? From her? He was the one who'd invited her out. The one who'd kissed her. And she'd scared him off just because she wanted him to coach her again?

But there was much more between them now than just that. She was crazy about this man. Had been for so long. Shannon didn't know why she'd gone looking for him today, except she hadn't stopped thinking about him all night and all day until finally she skipped her workout at the gym and drove out here.

Hudson yelled behind her again. Loud and clear. "Shannon. I'm sorry. Please stop!"

Smiling to herself, Shannon slowed, wanting to be caught by him, after all.

He skied next to her, and the terrain forced her concentration to the vertical slope. Hudson moved ahead of her and flew off a pile of packed snow. She followed, bracing herself for the land, then sliced the snow beside him.

Shannon couldn't remember ever having so much fun. They skied in rhythm. She and Hudson, they were good together, pushing the boundaries, as it were.

As the evergreens flashed by, she studied the slope in the distance, as she'd been trained to do, and noticed bushes littering her future—their future—if they continued on this path. Rocks emerged where there should have been snow, and there would have been, if this was a groomed run.

Shannon leaned to the side, cutting deep into the snow to break the downhill slide before it was too late. Hudson joined her.

Both of them stood motionless on their skis, breathless.

Heart in her throat, she stared at Hudson.

A pop snapped from somewhere above.

Hudson's expression slipped into shock.

"Snowslide! Come on!"

He skied at an angle, almost perpendicular to the slope. Panic carving over her heart, she followed. He wasn't trying to outrun the avalanche, but instead moved out of its path. The snow had started high above them, but moved at speeds to rival a downhill racer.

They had seconds to escape.

Pulse racing, she followed him. *Oh, dear Lord, help us!*

They weren't going to make it. The snow moved beneath her feet. Hudson caught her arm and, with superhuman strength, tugged her away from the collapsing snow. She held on to a tree, Hudson covering her, protecting her.

"Don't worry," he said over the roar of snow. "We're mostly out of the path."

Mostly?

Snow flowed over her, but he was right. It wasn't heavy. Finally, the slide settled. Shannon released her pent-up breath.

Once they'd moved from the center of the path, the tree had protected them. Hudson shook off what snow had found them.

"You okay?" He held her shoulders and looked her up and down.

Tears clogged her throat so she nodded. He must have read the emotion on her face and tugged her to him, holding her tight and secure.

"Thank you," she said against his chest. He'd saved them both. Shannon understood the dangers and knew what she was supposed to do, but that wasn't always possible. If it had been up to her, she would have tried to outrun it.

Finally, Hudson released her. "I've lost my skis. I could dig around for them, but I think the snow took them."

Shannon still had one. She huffed. "We'll have to hike to the bottom."

"I didn't see anyone else on this run. The avalanche stopped a ways down. Maybe we're the only ones."

"Do you think we triggered it?" She removed her helmet.

"I don't know." He ran his hand down her cheek, played with her hair that was all askew.

He scanned the mountain. They couldn't even see the lodge from here, of course, because they were on the wrong side. When his gaze drew back to her, his eyes dropped to her mouth. He leaned closer and pressed his forehead against hers.

"That was close," he whispered. "Way too close."

Then he pressed his lips against hers. Unlike last night, he didn't kiss her with a barely tethered passion. Instead his lips were soft and gentle, as if he cherished her as his most valuable possession.

Shannon thought her heart would burst.

He released her a little too abruptly. What was with him?

"You sure know how to show a girl a good time," she teased, needing some levity.

"It could take us a couple of hours to hike back to civilization," he said. "We could try to make it to another ski run within the boundaries. I have no idea if the ski patrol knows to look for us yet."

He tugged out his cell phone. "I can't call. No signal. But it'll cost if they come for us out here."

"Hudson." Shannon touched his arm. Even beneath his ski jacket, she could feel it. "You're shaking."

He dropped onto his backside in the snow.

"Are you okay?"

He rested his face in his gloved hands. "Sure."

Seeing Hudson like this startled her. He was like a rock. She didn't think anything ever got to him.

She sat in the snow next to him. "This your first avalanche?"

"Yeah. Yours?"

"What do you think?" She laughed, hoping to pull him out of his funk. It was strange being the strong one. "It was scary and exhilarating at the same time." She held out her hand. "I'm shaking, too."

Hudson still had his head in his hands. "Nothing exhilarating about it."

"All right. Look, I'm just trying to keep positive." Grabbing his biceps, she gave him a small shake. "Hudson, snap out of it. You're scaring me."

He sighed. Long and hard.

"Okay. Are you sure you're not hurt somewhere and you're just not telling me?" she asked. Maybe the answer was something deeper. Not physical at all.

Hudson blew out another breath and finally lifted his head, eyes shimmering. Shannon couldn't believe it.

"We could have been killed or hurt or maimed." He held her gaze.

"I know," she whispered.

"You're outside the protective boundaries of the ski resort because of me."

"Maybe Amanda will call the ski patrol for us."

"That's not what I mean."

In the distance, they heard snowmobiles. The ski patrol. Hudson stood up so they could be seen.

"I never told you about my sister."

Shannon's gut clenched as she recalled the moment when Coach Bradford had asked him about his sister. She'd had the feeling his question had been far from sincere. "No, you didn't. So…tell me."

"She had an injury. I convinced her to work through it. Push just a little harder because that had worked for me. I was too much of a daredevil. Took too many risks. Wasn't big on listening to the sports therapists with my own injuries. I thought she could handle it. I was an idiot."

Memories swept through her thoughts. "I remember all

the press—you were the miracle kid. That's why I didn't get your reason for making me hold back."

"The reason is simple. My sister fell. She has a spinal-cord injury. Can't use her legs. Because of me. I thought winning was everything, and that's why I can't coach you anymore. I can't be the reason. Not again. I can't watch you push harder and faster at death-defying speeds. I can't watch you get hurt."

The ski patrol approached, driving their snowmobiles right up to Shannon and Hudson.

Everything made sense now. *Oh, Hudson…* Shannon's knees buckled.

One of the ski-patrol guys scooped her onto the back of his snowmobile, ending anything more they could have said.

Chapter 15

The snowmobile carried Hudson back into the ski-resort boundaries, where they had taken great pains to keep the slopes safe from the threat of an avalanche.

Regret coursed through him as he held on to the guy who followed two other snowmobiles. Shannon rode the one in front.

He was done now. This had to be God's direction— Hudson had to let her go. He was no good for her and never had been. He'd made the right decision to leave, but maybe he hadn't gone far enough.

Snow clouds had moved in and hung thick in the sky, replacing the earlier brilliant blue, and echoed the heaviness pressing against his chest. If he loved her, and he admitted now that he did, he needed to walk away.

A half hour later, the ski-patrol snowmobiles drove right up to the lodge. They'd already assessed that Hudson and Shannon weren't in need of medical attention. The two were just glad to be safe. Hudson stepped off and shook the man's hand.

"Thanks, buddy." Hudson appreciated the ski patrol's assistance, but he wasn't looking forward to the stiff bill he would likely receive, since they'd had to travel outside the ski resort's boundaries.

"You're welcome, Landers. You might try listening to your own advice."

Shame flooded his being, squeezing his insides. How many lessons would he need before he learned?

Several gathered around him, Amanda grabbing his shoulders. "Are you all right?"

"Yeah. We're fine. Skied out of the way." *Mostly.*

Everyone had a question, but Hudson's attention was on Shannon, who had her own fan club. Unbelievably, her father had made it here and was now hugging her. News traveled fast. He must have already been in town to arrive so quickly. Hudson guessed Amanda had called him, too.

After he'd assured everyone that he was okay, Amanda tugged him aside. "You have some visitors."

Hudson stared. "Who?"

"They're inside. It was meant to be a surprise." Amanda looked guilty. She must have played a part in it.

Intrigued, Hudson pressed through the small gathering of relieved friends and entered the lodge in search of his visitors.

Amanda touched his arm. "Over there."

Hudson glanced across the great room. His little family from Texas huddled in the far corner. Jen sat in her chair along with their mother, talking to a Norwegian-looking guy.

Hudson's stomach clenched. He'd wanted her to come here to ski with him one day, hadn't he? This just wasn't the best day. He cut across the room. When his mother spotted him, her eyes grew wide along with her smile. Jen turned to face him, her smile growing, as well. That was when he saw her holding the guy's hand.

The guy stood when Hudson approached. "Mom. Jen. What are you doing here?"

"Aren't you glad to see us?" Jen asked.

"I told her we should have let you know," his mother offered.

"I wanted to surprise you."

"I'm surprised." Hudson leaned in to kiss her on the forehead.

His mother came around to hug him. "We heard you were nearly caught in an avalanche."

"Yes. But as you can see, I'm fine."

"And your friend Shannon was with you," Jen added.

At her name, his face sufffused with love for Shannon, but he couldn't allow things to go any further. Hudson hated that Jen could see right through him.

As if reading his unease, she tugged on his hand, letting him know that everything was okay.

"I came here to tell you the news in person," she said.

Hudson found the closest chair and dropped into it. He swallowed a lump. By the look on his sister's face, this couldn't be bad news, though. "What is it, Jen?"

She laughed. "You worry too much. I'm engaged." Jen held up her left hand, flaunting the huge diamond on her wedding finger.

The flaxen man stepped forward and thrust his hand out. "I'm Tim, by the way."

Overwhelmed with the news, Hudson suddenly found himself on his feet, shaking Tim's hand. This had all happened a little fast, hadn't it? "Jen mentioned there was someone special. I just thought…" He hadn't realized it would go this far.

Jen's smile faltered. "You thought what, that I would never find love again? Get married?"

The pain in her voice sliced right through him and twisted in his heart. "No, Jen. That's not it." He wasn't sure what it was anymore.

"So what? Ken left me because he couldn't handle what happened, but that doesn't banish me from love." Though Jen's voice was gentle, the pain in her eyes betrayed how Hudson had hurt her.

Hudson hated himself. He would rather die than hurt her, and yet he'd done just that. "Jen." Her name a whisper on his lips, he crouched to look her in the eye. "I couldn't be happier for you. For the both of you."

His kissed his sister's hand, as if she were a princess.

He stood and shook Tim's hand again. "Congratulations."

"Mom, will you and Tim please get us something to drink?" Jen asked.

Hudson's mother nodded, and Tim escorted her to the café. Alone time. Jen obviously had more to say. Hudson sat next to her. "So when's the big day?"

"Not for six months, at least. We're looking at dates, but I wanted you to be the first to know. After Mom and Dad, of course."

"Thank you for traveling all the way here just to tell me in person."

He squeezed her warm hand.

"It's more than that," she said. "I wanted you to see how happy I am. When you came to Texas, I got the feeling that you haven't moved on from the accident that left me like this. I've moved on, but you haven't. You're disabled. You're crippled, too, in a completely different way, but inside. You have to open up and live. Forgive yourself. Open up and...love again."

Hudson hung his head. She had gotten right to the crux of the matter, like always. Despite the crowd buzzing around him in the big lodge, dry sobs threatened. He had to contain them.

"Jen, you're hurt because of me. Shannon's injury, I'm to blame for that." He glanced behind him to make sure no one could hear and then leaned in. "And today. The avalanche. Shannon could have been killed because of me. It seems anyone I love is in danger when they're with me."

"That's ridiculous. People are better *because* of you. So you love adventure. You have a zeal for life and you don't hide that. Accidents happen and no one is to blame. I don't blame you. God has forgiven you, too, so who are you to hold yourself hostage?"

Her words convicted like a good sermon, both liberating and incriminating at the same time.

My grace is sufficient….

Jen's eyes shimmered. "Where is she, by the way?"

"Who? Shannon?"

"Yes, we were told they brought you both down the mountain. I want to meet her."

"Jen, no. Leave it. Whatever I had, or thought I had with her, needs to be over. It's for the best."

Wasn't it?

Shannon pressed her face into her father's shoulder and he held on tight.

Finally, she struggled from his embrace. "How did you know? How did you get here so fast?"

"I was in Santa Fe when Amanda called me."

"Amanda has your cell number?"

Her father's face colored. "Yes…I…"

"I thought you and Cecile were—" Shannon took a step back. "Wait a minute. You've been spying on me, haven't you? You want to know what I'm up to when I'm here working with Hudson."

Caught, her father spread his hands out. "I just want

to make sure you're okay. That you're not blowing your focus."

Shannon moved to press by him, her legs still shaking. He caught her arm.

"Don't walk away from me when I'm speaking to you."

She'd never been a disrespectful daughter. She and Daddy didn't have anyone else but each other. That was the way she'd always looked at it. But lately, she was feeling used by everyone around her. All she wanted to do was go home. Take a long, hot bath.

"What were you doing up there? With him? He's not your coach anymore."

"I wish he was. But you're right, he's not. I can't convince him to come back."

"You don't need him. Bradford's training works for you. I talked to him today, before I got the call you were here, and he says you're racing next weekend. One of the last races of the season. You hear that? You're *racing* again, Shannon. You wouldn't be racing again if Hudson was still your coach. Even if he's not coaching you, he's bad news. You don't need to endanger yourself or risk another injury. Stay away from him."

"What if I don't want to race anymore?" What would her father say to that? She'd brought that up before, so he shouldn't be surprised. Except…she would race next weekend? She wanted that more than anything.

His face reddened. "You don't know what you're saying. You're tired, Shannon. Let's go home."

She sagged. He was right. She'd put too much energy into getting to this point to give it all up. This was who she was. Even though she knew it was wrong to feel this way, she almost resented Hudson for introducing her to the disabled-skiers program. It only injected confusion into her struggle, because now she loved volunteering.

"Daddy, what if racing isn't what I'm meant to do?"

"What are you saying? It's Hudson, isn't it? He's been putting ideas in your head."

"I sometimes wonder if I wasn't racing, if anyone would care about me anymore."

Her father's face contorted. "How could you even think that?"

Easy.

"You mean everything to me." Her father looked twenty years older. "Even if you never set foot on a ski run again."

Though she'd hurt him, his reaction had given her what she needed.

The trembling started again. She wrapped her arms around herself. Her father squeezed her to him and started to walk with her. "Let's get you home. And do me a favor, please, just stay away from him."

They stepped forward and saw Hudson facing them. Though his features were stone, his eyes exposed his pain.

After a long, hot bath, Shannon dressed in her favorite sweater and stretchy pants. She planned to take it easy this evening. Stay home. Read a book. Think about Hudson and stay out of Coach Bradford's way.

At least for the time being.

She couldn't grasp that she would race next weekend—the first time in months since she'd taken the fall that had left her with serious injuries—but her experience today overshadowed any excitement she might have felt.

After they arrived at the cabin, Daddy informed her that Coach Bradford would be hard on her about today. She didn't relish facing him. Sitting on the sofa, she pulled her knees up and pressed her face into her hands.

Too many images accosted her, and they all involved Hudson. The worst one lingered in her mind, agony twisting in her heart. He'd been so hurt when her father had said those harsh words, then Shannon had allowed herself to be escorted to Daddy's car. He drove her home and paid some guys to bring her car later. It wasn't the right time to make a scene, and she'd had no energy. Besides, Hudson had left her with the impression he wanted her to stay away from him. That she wasn't safe if she was with him. She wasn't even sure he still wanted her to volunteer.

But her heart screamed it was all wrong.

An enormous weight pressed down on her—she had to race, to win. People were counting on her. She wasn't loved if she didn't deliver what was expected of her. She'd already lost Jack for that reason.

If she didn't race, she'd lose Daddy's respect, if not his love, and so much more would go wrong.

And then there was the enigma named Hudson Landers. He was the exact opposite. He wouldn't love her if she *continued* to race. At least while her knee was in question. But it was obviously much more than that with him. Like her father said, he had issues.

She closed her eyes and relaxed into the pillow on the sofa, remembering the kiss. She'd kind of wanted another one today, and she had already hoped to get one at the bottom of the slope after their exhilarating, crazy run out of bounds, but then the snow had given way and changed their course.

Their day.

Maybe even their lives.

And then Hudson had kissed her as if she meant the world to him.

Daddy had no idea what he was asking when he told her to stay away from Hudson.

I love him.

She realized that now.

She hadn't said the words, but couldn't her father see that? Didn't he know her well enough? Or was he too caught up in his plans for her life? Or maybe Daddy did see her feelings clearly, and that was why he demanded all the more that she stay clear of Hudson.

Downhill ski racing had been her dream. The plan for her life. What she was made for. And yet, the price was so very high.

Someone knocked on the front door.

Oh, no. Coach Bradford.

Shannon scraped her hair back into a ponytail. Couldn't the man give it a day? She'd been through a lot.

She opened the door.

Hudson.

Chapter 16

"I didn't expect to see you," she said. "You look like a wreck."

"Thanks."

"Anytime." She grinned and opened the door for him.

With damp hair slicked back and wearing a sweater and stretchy pants, she was more beautiful than ever. An image of her in her lavender dress came to mind. The Flurry Fundraiser seemed a lifetime ago.

His stomach suddenly dropped. "Are you sure it's okay for me to come in?"

She arched a brow. "You saying you came over to stand on my porch?"

Hudson scraped his hand down his jaw. "I just need a few minutes to talk. It won't take long."

"I suppose you know Daddy isn't home, or you wouldn't be here."

"I didn't know. His presence wouldn't have kept me from coming."

"Then step right in."

He entered the cozy cabin, brushing by Shannon and breathing in her light floral shampoo. He jammed his hands into his pockets. He'd never stepped foot in the cabin before.

"Have a seat," she said. "Can I get you something to drink?"

"No, I'm good." Hudson chose the plush burgundy side chair.

"Okay, well, if you don't mind, I'm getting hot chocolate."

"I don't."

A fire blazed in the potbellied stove, making the room warm and comfortable, and with exhaustion creeping over him, Hudson knew he might fall asleep if he wasn't careful. He had business to take care of.

Steaming mug in hand, Shannon made her way to the sofa and sank deep into the corner. She slurped the hot liquid and eyed him over the rim.

Hudson gripped the armrests, feeling uneasy. But he had to do this.

Shannon shifted forward. "I'm sorry about what my father said. I know you heard him. Is that why you're here?"

"Yes and no."

This was it. He was really going to do this. "He was right. You should stay away from me."

"And yet you came to see *me*." She hung her head, angling it a little.

"What I told you up on the mountain—I have a way of hurting the people I love." Had he really just said the word *love?* "Care about deeply," he added to tone down the stronger word. But did she already know how strongly he felt?

"That's what you came over to tell me?"

"No. You brought up your father. I was just agreeing."

"Then what?" Anger seeped into her tone.

"I heard that you start racing next weekend."

"We're back to that again. You telling me it's too soon."

"I want to make sure that it's what you really want. That you're not being pressured because everyone expects it from you. I know the feeling. I remember it well. If you are, just tell me. I won't hesitate to say something. If Bradford doesn't know about your knee, he needs to be informed."

A soft smile edged into her lips. "I appreciate that you'd go to bat for me like that, Hudson, even when you're not my coach. You sure you don't want to come back?"

He chuckled, hanging his head. If he didn't have his own baggage, he'd do it in a minute. He had to be the only coach with so many reservations, but maybe he wasn't alone in his experience.

"You know I can't. You know why." He drew in a breath of courage. "Let me try this again. Please, Shannon. Don't race. You'll end up driving yourself too hard. The stakes are too high, the competition relentless. I've already told you this too many times to count. If you aren't completely healed, racing too soon could end your career for good." He stared into the flames of the stove. "Or worse." Those last words were a whispered creak.

Shannon drew in a long breath, but she didn't say anything. With a thoughtful expression, she stirred her cup of hot chocolate. "You came over to confirm to me that I should stay away from you, but if I didn't want to ski in the race, you'd step in and speak to my coach and my father. And in the end, you're begging me not to race. Anything else? Or is that all?"

"When you put it that way, well, yes, that's about all."

And he sounded like an idiot. Shannon put her cup down and stood, edging her way toward him. Hudson rose, as well. She must be about to usher him out the door. He deserved it.

He turned to oblige, but she caught his arm and stopped him. Looking up at him, she was too close. "Everyone is counting on me to race. You're hoping I won't. I'm more than a body attached to skis, Hudson Landers. Much more than that, you know?"

Her hazel-green eyes glistened in the much too cozy room. The ambience was nothing if not romantic.

A knot swelled in his throat.

Her smile enticing, she wanted him to know that she was all woman. He'd never doubted that. Why was she doing this to him? Torturing him like this?

"I came here today—"

"—to end us before we even started and to offer me help at the same time?" Her soft chuckle was incredulous. "When we were on the slopes together today, before the avalanche, all I could think about was how well we skied together. How well we worked and played together. How much…how much I wanted you to kiss me again."

His restraint failed. Hudson grabbed her to him, and she pressed eagerly into his arms, into his lips.

Shannon. Beautiful Shannon.

This wasn't supposed to happen. He needed to set things straight. But instead he found himself weaving his hands through her thick auburn hair, tugging out her ponytail so he could feel the silky strands of her long mane between his fingers. Her lips were soft and tender, and the woman inside was strong and full of passion for life and others. For him.

He slid his hands around her back now, tugging her nice and close. How he loved her. And that was exactly why he had to let her go.

Ending the kiss, he pressed into a hug, feeling the ache of regret to his bones. He wanted something he just couldn't have. Shannon would never listen to his instruction, because she wasn't created to hold anything back. She was more like Hudson than he wanted to admit.

The door swung open. "What's this?"

Shannon's father stood in the doorway.

Hudson took three steps back and bumped into the chair behind him.

"Hi, Daddy. Hudson stopped by to tell me how sorry he was about today. And to offer his congratulations that I'm scheduled to race next weekend." Shannon injected happiness into her voice. She didn't need Daddy exploding, messing everything up.

Good thing he hadn't walked in and seen them kissing.

Holding two sacks of groceries, he kicked the door shut behind him and headed to the table to set them down. "Looked like more than that to me."

"A goodbye hug, that's all."

Nervous like a schoolboy caught doing something wrong, Hudson scraped his hand through his hair. "Robert, I don't think Shannon's ready for that race."

"What did you say?"

Now Daddy was flat-out angry.

"Her knee still bothers her. Did you know that? You send her in too early and she could get hurt in a big way."

What are you doing? Sending a glare at Hudson, Shannon stepped between them, but it didn't matter.

"This coming from the man who almost got her killed today."

"Whoa, Daddy. That was all my fault. He didn't invite me. I followed him."

Her father ignored her, but she knew she'd hear more from him about that later.

"She has a coach, Landers, and you're not it." Daddy pressed his hands on his hips. "I think you should leave, and make sure it's for good this time."

Hudson pursed his lips, nodded and left through the front door.

Shannon turned on her father. "My life is my decision. The race is my decision. And my relationship with Hudson is also my decision."

She ran out the door and after Hudson in her bare feet. "Hudson!"

He'd made fast tracks across the snow-covered lawn and had already reached the parking lot. Shannon ran after him.

"Hudson! Wait!" How many times would she chase after this man?

He ignored her and kept walking. Her feet freezing, her body shivering, she finally caught up with him.

He stared down at her, taking in her exposed form. "What are you doing?"

"Chasing after you like always. What does it look like?"

He frowned. "Go home."

"I wasn't finished talking when Daddy interrupted us."

Shaking his head, he unlocked his Explorer. "Get in."

"With pleasure." Shannon scrambled in on the other side, hoping for some warmth.

Hudson climbed in and turned on the ignition.

"Heat please."

"Working on it."

He angled his head and grinned. "Your father might show up and yank you out."

"I told him to leave us alone. I'm a big girl. He knows that. He just gets crazy where you're concerned. I don't know why."

"I do."

"Yeah, I think I do, too."

Shannon was in love with Hudson, and Daddy knew it. He was afraid that his life's work—his daughter's skiing career—was about to be buried in a snowslide. That she was about to give in to the distractions of life.

And honestly, she wanted to. More than anything. But a part of her burned to do what she was born to do.

Hudson blew out a breath.

She couldn't help herself. She reached over and ran her fingers through his thick, dark hair just like she'd wanted to do for so long. Too long. He didn't fight her touch, but instead relaxed into it and leaned against the headrest. They were meant to be together, so she couldn't understand why it was this hard.

Shannon wanted to climb over the console to be next to Hudson, but that was awkward. She leaned closer and touched his cheek, then pressed her face close to his. "I have to do this. I have to race. I'm not doing it for anyone but me. If anyone can understand that, you can."

"I do."

"But you're not going to come watch the race, are you?"

"We're not good for each other. Maybe if I didn't blame myself for things, it would be different. But I can't give you what you want, what you need."

"You're wrong. You've helped me to figure out who I am," she whispered, tears sliding down her cheeks. "I...I think I love you, Hudson."

He grasped her wrists then, forcing some distance between them. "Don't make this harder for either of us. Don't say things you don't mean or can't follow through with."

A sob caught in her throat. How could he be so cruel? Maybe Daddy was right all along.

Chapter 17

If he hadn't been occupied with assisting Jen in the bi-ski, Hudson might have gone crazy.

Shannon was in Aspen and would race tomorrow. He thought he'd let her go. He'd certainly released his coaching responsibilities, giving up any right to intrude into her life, especially since he'd shut down her talk of love.

When she'd confessed her feelings, it should have been a special moment, and he'd ruined it for her. For them both. He'd been heartsick ever since that night.

Jen had tried to coax what happened out of him, but he couldn't talk about it.

But now Jen let out a squeal of delight, drawing his focus back to his sister. Though he gripped the tethers that attached to the bi-ski and followed behind, Jen would certainly progress to the point where she wouldn't need this kind of assistance.

Their mother and Tim had traveled back to Texas to

keep their commitments, while Jen had stayed on for a few days longer to experience skiing once again.

At the bottom of the slope, Hudson helped her stop the ski, and he came around to stand in front of her. He wanted to see the look on her face.

And that look told him everything words could not.

"Oh, Hudson!" Her eyes shined brighter than he ever remembered seeing. "Thank you for this. It's more than I could have imagined." Tears streaked down her cheeks to her smile.

He released his ski boots from the skis and knelt by her. "What's the matter? Are you okay?"

She laughed. "I've never been better."

While relieved to hear that, glad her experience had gone as he'd hoped, he knew that her words weren't true. She *had* been better. Back when she had the use of her legs.

Hudson stood, hoping she wouldn't catch the despair behind his eyes.

She wiped at the moisture on her cheeks. "I wish Tim could have been here to see."

"Me, too," Hudson said.

"I'm glad you're doing this work, Hudson. It suits you." She paused, a look in her eyes that told him there was more. "Don't get me wrong, but you're not the reason I'm here. If it weren't for Tim, I doubt I'd be here today."

Hudson thought he'd been the one to bring her. "How so?"

"I doubt I'd have the courage to come." Jen had one of those deep expressions on her face. "He helped me to understand that life is a risk and if you're not willing to risk, then you're not willing to live. That's true for love, too. Tim helped me to know I could love again and be loved."

Unable to hold her gaze, he focused on the other volunteers.

"You're the guy who wasn't afraid of anything, who took the ski world by storm with your risk taking. I would have followed you anywhere, but I won't follow you to this dark place you've chosen. I never thought you would be such a coward."

That jerked his attention back. He stared at her, feeling the stab of her words. How could his gentle, loving sister be so harsh?

He couldn't breathe, much less respond.

"And now you're too afraid to love, and you're existence is no life at all."

"How can you say that?"

The tears came afresh, and this time there wasn't a smile. "Because I love you. What kind of a sister would I be if I didn't tell you the truth? I've watched you all week, living in misery because you love that girl. I'm sorry I didn't tell you sooner, or at least wait for a better time, but it's been hard holding it in."

Now he was the one paralyzed. With fear and guilt.

My grace is sufficient....

Moisture built in the corner of his eyes as he saw the truth of it. "How do I fix any of it? I can't."

He wanted to drop to his knees. He was weak, so weak.

But, God, you are strong when I am weak.

Jen had slipped her glove off and gripped his hand. "Yes, you *can* fix this. You let her go when you should have let the blame go. Just switch it up. Let go of your self-imprisonment and go after her. Don't be afraid to love her and let her be who she is."

Jen had always been his rock, and she had never stopped. He smiled as he realized she was right.

A lone tear escaped. "Let's get you back to the lodge," he said. "I have a plane to catch."

* * *

Up next, Shannon waited at the gate.

Her breaths came too fast. Nerves tingling all over, her palms grew slick inside her gloves. She reminded herself this wasn't anything like the last time she'd raced. They'd been allowed an inspection ski of the course to get familiar for the downhill race.

When taking the fall months ago, she feared it would end her world, but here she was again.

Closing her eyes, she prayed.

God, be with me today. I've learned a lot since my last race. That it's okay if I don't ever race again, and it's okay if I do because You're with me, no matter what. And Daddy loves me no matter what I decide to do with my life.... And Hudson...

A pang shot through her insides.

Help him forgive himself.

Tears threatened to fall as she recalled the moment he'd thrown her profession of love back in her face. She opened her eyes and sucked in a cold breath.

She was up.

At this height, the snow-covered Rockies were spread before her. Shannon stabbed her poles into the white stuff, getting into position at the start gate. Racing again was like a new dream. A dream that had eluded her for too long. In this new dream, winning today wouldn't matter, because there would be another race.

But she had one chance at this. A single run down the slope. Topping speeds between 80 and 100 mph, in one minute and thirty seconds—if she was fast enough—it would all be over.

It would be the longest two minutes of her life.

Sucking in a breath, she concentrated on the downhill course that would wind and pitch and throw her off, if she let it. But this wasn't anything she hadn't done a thousand times before. The downhill event was all about speed. Except this time, for Shannon, it was about the simple fact that she was here. Racing again. The only thing missing was that Hudson wasn't here to watch.

The starter counted down the last five seconds.

Five, four, three, two... The horn resounded, and Shannon plunged forward.

After a harrowing travel experience, Hudson was afraid he would miss Shannon's race altogether. But he'd made it to the ski-racing complex with half an hour to spare. With the Women's Giant Slalom coming to a close, the crowd had dispersed and then reassembled. Hudson had found the perfect place from which to watch Shannon in the downhill.

He could have positioned himself near the gate, but he knew that if she saw him there, that could throw off her focus. The bottom of the ski run was best. That way, when Shannon finished, Hudson would be there to greet her. He smiled at the thought, though he wasn't sure of her reception. He didn't care about Bradford's reaction, or too much about her father's, who had to be in attendance, considering this was an important race for Shannon.

He sent up a prayer to God, thanking Him that he had finally seen where he needed to be, before it was too late. The sports announcer rambled on about Shannon's speed and form and how this was her first race since her fall, and he added that she'd been through several coaches.

Then he saw her. Her slender, athletic form tucked deep and perfect in the fall line to become as aerodynamic as possible. *Good girl!*

Shannon flew over the last jump and leaned to her left so far that her hand scraped through the snow. Was this it? Would she fall, her knee showing weakness? His pulse roared in his ears.

Please, God, don't let her fall again. Let her adapt.

The scene was like déjà vu, but Hudson wouldn't look away, even though he'd told her he couldn't watch. He would be there for her, and this time he wouldn't leave. He should have helped her with her dream. He should have found a way.

Shannon righted herself and her left ski flew off. She sped through the finish line on one ski.

Hudson threw his arms up and shouted for joy.

That had cost her precious seconds, but it didn't matter.

Hudson tore from the crowd to meet her as she slowed at the bottom, coming to a stop, and then she skied over to the sidelines. But he wasn't alone in his eagerness to see her. Her father embraced her, as did Cecile, who held Robert's hand. Bradford was still up at the top and would remain there through Piper's race.

Then Shannon's father saw Hudson approaching. To his surprise, her father gave him a warm smile and offered his hand. "I hoped you would make it."

Huh?

Shannon's eyes grew wide but her smile won the day. She broke from her skis and threw her arms around his neck—something he didn't expect.

"Oh, Hudson, you made it."

He hadn't realized she had wanted him there. "I wouldn't have missed it for the world." And that was the truth, once he got over himself.

"That means everything to me." She released him. "This is the best day of my life. I wanted to race again, but even if I had won, it would have meant nothing if you hadn't been here with me. Someone once told me that winning isn't everything."

Hudson was taken aback. He didn't think she had seriously considered his position about her racing. Missing the feel of her arms around his neck, he tugged her toward him again and cupped her face. He took in the fiery excitement in her eyes. How did he think he could ever live without her?

"I want to be there for all your races. I'm sorry that I let you down. And…I'm sorry that you were the first one to say 'I love you.'"

Hudson leaned in and kissed her, knowing he couldn't take all the time in the world like he wanted—people were watching. But he wanted the kiss to convey everything. Her response told him that it did, except there was one more thing.

When he eased away, he whispered, "I love you, Shannon. I have for a long time, and I wish it hadn't taken me this long to tell you. So I'm not going to take my time with this—will you marry me?"

Tears streamed from her eyes. "I only thought this was the happiest day of my life. Yes, Hudson. Yes. All I ever wanted was to be on your team."

* * * * *

REQUEST YOUR FREE BOOKS!

2 FREE INSPIRATIONAL NOVELS
PLUS 2
FREE
MYSTERY GIFTS

Love Inspired

YES! Please send me 2 FREE Love Inspired® novels and my 2 FREE mystery gifts (gifts are worth about $10). After receiving them, if I don't wish to receive any more books, I can return the shipping statement marked "cancel." If I don't cancel, I will receive 6 brand-new novels every month and be billed just $4.74 per book in the U.S. or $5.24 per book in Canada. That's a savings of at least 21% off the cover price. It's quite a bargain! Shipping and handling is just 50¢ per book in the U.S. and 75¢ per book in Canada.* I understand that accepting the 2 free books and gifts places me under no obligation to buy anything. I can always return a shipment and cancel at any time. Even if I never buy another book, the two free books and gifts are mine to keep forever.

105/305 IDN F49N

Name _____ (PLEASE PRINT)

Address _____ Apt. #

City _____ State/Prov. _____ Zip/Postal Code

Signature (if under 18, a parent or guardian must sign)

Mail to the **Harlequin® Reader Service:**
IN U.S.A.: P.O. Box 1867, Buffalo, NY 14240-1867
IN CANADA: P.O. Box 609, Fort Erie, Ontario L2A 5X3

**Are you a subscriber to Love Inspired books
and want to receive the larger-print edition?
Call 1-800-873-8635 or visit www.ReaderService.com.**

* Terms and prices subject to change without notice. Prices do not include applicable taxes. Sales tax applicable in N.Y. Canadian residents will be charged applicable taxes. Offer not valid in Quebec. This offer is limited to one order per household. Not valid for current subscribers to Love Inspired books. All orders subject to credit approval. Credit or debit balances in a customer's account(s) may be offset by any other outstanding balance owed by or to the customer. Please allow 4 to 6 weeks for delivery. Offer available while quantities last.

Your Privacy—The Harlequin® Reader Service is committed to protecting your privacy. Our Privacy Policy is available online at www.ReaderService.com or upon request from the Harlequin Reader Service.

We make a portion of our mailing list available to reputable third parties that offer products we believe may interest you. If you prefer that we not exchange your name with third parties, or if you wish to clarify or modify your communication preferences, please visit us at www.ReaderService.com/consumerchoice or write to us at Harlequin Reader Service Preference Service, P.O. Box 9062, Buffalo, NY 14269. Include your complete name and address.

LIDIR13R

REQUEST YOUR FREE BOOKS!

2 FREE INSPIRATIONAL NOVELS
PLUS 2
FREE
MYSTERY GIFTS

Love Inspired.
HISTORICAL
INSPIRATIONAL HISTORICAL ROMANCE

YES! Please send me 2 FREE Love Inspired® Historical novels and my 2 FREE mystery gifts (gifts are worth about $10). After receiving them, if I don't wish to receive any more books, I can return the shipping statement marked "cancel." If I don't cancel, I will receive 4 brand-new novels every month and be billed just $4.74 per book in the U.S. or $5.24 per book in Canada. That's a savings of at least 21% off the cover price. It's quite a bargain! Shipping and handling is just 50¢ per book in the U.S. and 75¢ per book in Canada.* I understand that accepting the 2 free books and gifts places me under no obligation to buy anything. I can always return a shipment and cancel at any time. Even if I never buy another book, the two free books and gifts are mine to keep forever.

102/302 IDN F5CY

Name	(PLEASE PRINT)	
Address		Apt. #
City	State/Prov.	Zip/Postal Code

Signature (if under 18, a parent or guardian must sign)

Mail to the Harlequin® Reader Service:
IN U.S.A.: P.O. Box 1867, Buffalo, NY 14240-1867
IN CANADA: P.O. Box 609, Fort Erie, Ontario L2A 5X3

Want to try two free books from another series?
Call 1-800-873-8635 or visit www.ReaderService.com.

* Terms and prices subject to change without notice. Prices do not include applicable taxes. Sales tax applicable in N.Y. Canadian residents will be charged applicable taxes. Offer not valid in Quebec. This offer is limited to one order per household. Not valid for current subscribers to Love Inspired Historical books. All orders subject to credit approval. Credit or debit balances in a customer's account(s) may be offset by any other outstanding balance owed by or to the customer. Please allow 4 to 6 weeks for delivery. Offer available while quantities last.

Your Privacy—The Harlequin® Reader Service is committed to protecting your privacy. Our Privacy Policy is available online at www.ReaderService.com or upon request from the Harlequin Reader Service.

We make a portion of our mailing list available to reputable third parties that offer products we believe may interest you. If you prefer that we not exchange your name with third parties, or if you wish to clarify or modify your communication preferences, please visit us at www.ReaderService.com/consumerschoice or write to us at Harlequin Reader Service Preference Service, P.O. Box 9062, Buffalo, NY 14269. Include your complete name and address.

LIHDIR13R

Reader Service.com

Manage your account online!

- Review your order history
- Manage your payments
- Update your address

---

*We've designed
the Harlequin® Reader Service
website just for you.*

Enjoy all the features!

- Reader excerpts from any series
- Respond to mailings and
  special monthly offers
- Discover new series available to you
- Browse the Bonus Bucks catalog
- Share your feedback

Visit us at:

ReaderService.com